~

'Manjushree Thapa's stories fall into the category that the Japanese call "palm-of-the-hand" stories. Some of them are just a page long, delicate or witty sketches that trace a mood, or a moment [...] Thapa's skill is in evoking the passage of time and recording tectonic shifts of cultural disruption with an eye that is both clinical and as delicate as the flutter of a butterfly's wings [...] There is both a sense of despair and celebration that is brilliantly balanced.'—*India Today*

'Not a single story in this collection disappoints. The writing is simple and uncluttered, unlike the lives of some of Thapa's characters and in contrast to the changes Nepal has experienced in recent years [...] *Tilled Earth* is a quiet, thoughtful collection of stories; nothing dramatic or melodramatic, but intense nonetheless.'—SAWNET Book Reviews

'Thapa's characters are refreshingly real, and her writing is entertaining [...] The crispness of her tone and her gentle humour speak volumes for her self-assurance as a writer. Her people—old woodworkers, retired babus, lyricist-politicians, engineers, feminists, NGO employees, old Civil Servants and American Leftists—are all etched in precisely, with fondness and dignity.'—*Time Out*

'Some of [Thapa's] short stories beautifully evoke an entire world in just one or two paragraphs [...] Thapa's irony [can be] crushing, but it is when she leaves some channel of redemption open for her characters that *Tilled Earth* is most satisfying.'—*Mint*

~

TILLED EARTH

Stories

MANJUSHREE THAPA

ALEPH

ALEPH

ALEPH BOOK COMPANY
An independent publishing firm
promoted by *Rupa Publications India*

Published in 2012 by
Aleph Book Company
7/16 Ansari Road, Daryaganj
New Delhi 110002

First published in India by Penguin Books India 2007

ISBN: 978-93-822775-1-4

1 3 5 7 9 10 8 6 4 2

For sale in the Indian subcontinent only.

Typeset in Adobe Garamond Pro by SÜRYA, New Delhi

Printed by Replika Press Pvt. Ltd
Kundli, Haryana

For Tsoknyi Rinpoche
whose kindness is immeasurable

For discourse (and therefore, for man) nothing is more frightening than the *absence of answer*.

—Mikhail Bakhtin

Contents

~

~

Heera Maharjan Loses His Way

~

Heera Maharjan, in his time a prolific woodworker, took the old temple road but turned at the wrong traffic light and suddenly found himself in a neighbourhood of walls. Brick, brick, concrete, brick. All the old rice fields had been overlaid with construction. Though Heera had grown up not far from here, he no longer recognized this land. How many of the door and window frames here, the cupboards and closets and racks, had been built by his hands? They all disappeared into the city—. The path in front of him wound up to a high metal gate. Through the clouds of his cataract-covered vision, Heera saw green tips of ivy at the sides of the gate. He could smell sweet peas in bloom in the garden beyond. A pearl-white butterfly fluttered past him. He went up to the gate and peered in through a crack. The garden beyond had been landscaped to perfection, like the gardens in films or on television: ethereal. There were crocuses lined up in beds, and snapdragons, lilies, roses planted at the feet of a jacaranda tree. There was a row of plants with frilled yellow petals, delicate stems and dark purple leaves. He did not know their name. He recognized the geraniums: Germany flowers. And there were gardenia bushes and rows of succulent

11

jade along an immaculate lawn dappled with light. The May winds stirred, unloosening jacaranda buds from the tree, and Heera pressed into the gate as if to receive their blessing. He heard himself say Mother. Then he stepped back and looked around. Brick and concrete. How to get back to the old temple road? He did not want to be late for the feast offered on this day, once a year, on the death anniversary of his former patron Sridhar Jung Rana, a man of such infinite fortune it was said he had owned a house in all seventy-five districts of the country.

Soar

~

Putting the water to boil, Nadia remembered that she was supposed
to call someone about something, but she couldn't remember
who or about what. Was it a gender specialist for next week's
women's rights seminar? About trafficking, rape, child
prostitution, domestic abuse, the lack of basic rights for Nepali
women? This hangover was killing her. With shaking hands she
picked up the day's *Kathmandu Post* and scanned the headlines
before turning, slowly, to the back pages. There was nothing
much in the international news. When she heard the kettle hiss
she put down the paper and with some effort made a pot of
coffee. She took a cup to the living room, along with the paper.
Instead of reading it she examined a potted banyan plant she
had bought the previous week. A few fresh leaves had uncurled
overnight: delicate and moist, vulnerable. Under her breath she
sang to them: 'Shall I soar above these hills and peaks?' It was a
folk song she had learned on a trek a few months after coming
to Nepal, when she believed there were simple solutions to
simple problems. 'These hills and peaks,' she broke off. She
didn't know the rest of the words. She lifted the coffee to her
lips but it was too hot to drink. For a while she looked at the

corner of the window ledge, where the egg sacs of spiders had appeared a few weeks back. When would the eggs hatch? She looked awhile at their silky bundles. Then she went back to rereading *The Kathmandu Post*. The local news was in fine print on the third page. Woman, she read. Woman Considered Witch Forced to Eat Faeces by Villagers. She put the paper aside and gulped down her coffee.

At lunch Nadia flipped through brochures for package holidays to Pattaya, Colombo, Goa. Blue waters, white sand. She thought: one gets so wrapped up in the woes of this country, one forgets how easy it is to leave. An hour's flight to Delhi, three to Hong Kong and eighteen to the apartment she had given up in Brooklyn eighteen months ago.

When she got home from work that evening she found the maid standing on a window ledge, dusting a hard-to-reach corner. It always surprised her how Nepali women could manage in saris: all those pleats and folds did not seem to trip them up. There was such—resilience—in Nepali women. The maid was lithe despite being middle aged. Nimbly, she stretched across the window ledge and, as Nadia watched on, she reached for the spiders' egg sacs and picked them off with one deft pinch, killing the larvae inside.

That night Nadia got through a bottle of Shiraz scanning United Nations manuals on evacuation provisions in case of emergency.

Solitaire

~

Hit Bahadur Khadka had discovered solitaire on the computer, and he was spending his last days at the Ministry of Home Affairs shuffling the deck whenever the hand seemed unfavourable. Late in life perhaps. Years he had worked as a clerk, writing each visitor's name on a slip, taking it in to the latest minister—'Someone is hoping to meet His Excellency'— and returning to his office with its tatty jute carpet and paint peeling off the walls, its lumpy sofa and stained curtains, its sole rickety desk now boasting a brand new Korean computer. Democracy had come and gone and come again over the span of his career. Movements had started; a war had been fought. Scores of ministers had passed through his life. Nineteen and a half years he had waited for visitors. He had a mere six months left till retirement. He was learning to play solitaire on the computer, late in life perhaps.

Sounds That the Tongue Learns to Make

~

Do you speak English? I only speak a little Nepali. I do not
understand. Please say it again. Please speak more slowly.
What is your name? How old are you? Where do you live?
Are your parents alive? Are you married? How many
brothers do you have? How many sisters? How many in
your family? How many children?

The rock was warm against Sarah's palm, its surface an even,
luminous grey, and smooth, worn down by travellers who must
have, like her, brushed by or leaned against it, seeking support.
The sky above her was hazy, the air flecked with dust. She could
hear the distant rush of a river she could not see. The sweat on
her upper lips trickled into her mouth. She had only three
changes of clothes in her pack, but the weight was heavy on her
shoulders. Her neck was already sore.

Keshab was sauntering ahead, overtaking a group of local
women dressed in festive red and pink saris. The women were
talking loudly and carrying in their hands offerings of flowers
and grains. They must be on their way to a temple, Sarah
thought. One woman stopped to pluck a bellflower from a vine

along the trail, deftly pushing the flower into her braids, before fixing the pleats of her sari and scampering off to catch up with the others. Keshab was beyond the group by then, no longer visible on the trail.

Sarah pushed herself off the rock. Her hiking boots were heavy. Ahead, the Nepali woman's bellflower bounced in her hair.

It had been her idea, this trek, something she had wanted to do to mark the end of her tenure in Nepal. Soon after their first embrace, she had suggested it to Keshab: 'We should trek the Himalayas together.' She had heard from all the expats in Kathmandu that this trail was safe. There were no Maoists here. And it was easy. Forty thousand foreigners a year stayed in the lodges, eating at tea shops: how hard could it possibly be? They wouldn't have to carry tents or food.

Keshab had not been enthusiastic, initially. 'People like us who grew up in the hills…' For her benefit, he always enunciated soft Nepali djas and tas with special emphasis: haami jasto gaunma hurkekaaharu… His opinion had carried through his wry tone: it was indulgent to trek for leisure through villages where people were so poor. Keshab was a socialist; he had been active in the student unions in college. Sarah had not known him to take holidays, or even days off from work. But then, a week ago, he had suggested that they take off to the hills. Not to the east, where he had grown up: too many people knew him there, he said. She would be leaving soon. He had said it would be good for them to have some time alone.

Sarah turned a bend in the path and found him waiting there. He turned to her, smiling. He hadn't even broken a sweat. She came up to him, slightly out of breath. She was his height, with the same large-boned build. When she stood by him their eyes were level. She was too big to ever pass for a Nepali, though her complexion was tanned and her hair dark.

'You are enjoying?' Keshab reached out for her hands, surprising her. In Kathmandu they were circumspect about touching each other in public. He said, 'It is not far now.' Dropping her hands, he started off again. The trail led towards a village clustered along a riverbank. That must be the village—Sarah couldn't remember its name—where they were supposed to stay the night. She followed him.

The lodge they chose, the first one along the trail, was a small house with clay walls and a slate roof. Inside, flimsy wood partitions separated one room from another and from a sooty kitchen, from where came the noise of pots, pans and kitchen utensils being put to use. An elderly French couple was occupying the best room in the lodge. 'This is a dormitory room,' the woman of the lodge said in mixed Nepali and English, leading them to a room with a row of beds. She stood with her feet flat apart and looked frankly from Keshab to Sarah back to Keshab. 'There's also a double room upstairs.'

'We'll stay in that one,' he said.

The woman seemed to wince, but she led them up a stairway to an attic room. 'There's water for washing in the kitchen,' she said to Keshab, in Nepali. 'The toilets are outside. There's a solar water heater for showers.' She lowered her voice. 'Is the woman American?'

Sarah responded for him. 'Ma American ho.'

Keshab corrected her: 'Ma American hun.'

The lodge keeper again looked from one to the other.

Relaxing over a beer that evening, and enjoying the promise of the week ahead, Sarah sat on the porch—avoiding the elderly French couple, who kept glancing over as though wanting to talk—and watched some local men trapping logs in the river. The hills nearby were blocking the view of the Annapurna range. The village houses were sturdy, of stone and slate. The fields beyond were thick with wheat. Sarah knew she should resist images of idyll—the country's per capita income was dismal, for god's sake. Areas like these lacked even the most rudimentary services. The literacy rate was thirty per cent nationally, and seventeen per cent for women. One had to keep all this in sight.

Nearby, Keshab was asking the lodge owner about her infant son: 'Kati barsa bhayo?'

She loved to listen to him talking. Kati. Silently, Sarah mouthed the soft ta that didn't exist in English. 'Barsa': the purr of the ra. How many years old?

Ka kha ga gha nga. Sounds that her tongue had learned to make this year.

Early the next morning, Keshab reached over and whispered for her to wake up. She felt him slip out of bed and the next thing she knew, he was calling out her name again. 'Saa'rah. Saa'rah.' He had told her that in Nepali her name meant entirety; he often strung the word into a sentence that said she was his entire world. Timi mero saa'rah sansar hau. His hands were cool on her face. He said, 'It is so late already. I have asked for the meals. Omelettes will make you strong for walking. Your tea will get so cold. You must wake now and let us go.'

She rose, packed and went down to wash her face at a bucket of water in the kitchen. Keshab was sitting on the porch. She joined him there for a pot of mint tea and a chewy cheese omelette. The first silver rays of sunlight disappeared behind a gathering of clouds. The morning air was dewy.

Keshab had taken some of Sarah's money at the start of the trip. Now he went into the kitchen to pay their bills. Sarah worried that the things they did together sometimes cost more than he could afford. Her consultancy fees came to over two hundred thousand rupees a month, more than Keshab made in a year, or maybe a year and a half—she had never asked how much he earned as a language instructor. He supplemented his income by offering tuition to high-school students. And he was a moderately reputed novelist, though he likely earned a meagre pittance from his novels. Sarah did not consider it fair to expect him to split their costs halfway.

Keshab came out from the kitchen with his pack already strapped on. 'Let us follow the river to Ulleri,' he said, and started off.

Sarah's calves felt tight from yesterday's walk, but she tried not to lag behind. Beyond the village, the trail sloped up along a hillside, into a sparse broadleaf forest. She stepped carefully through the mossy clefts and rocks. Keshab, well ahead of her, would from time to time wait for her; but every time she was about to catch up, he would head off again. Sarah would have preferred to walk together, but she didn't want to ask him to slow down just for her. That would seem needy.

So she walked alone, feeling big and out of shape, telling herself that in a day or two, her body would get used to this toil.

Or that was what had happened on the only other trek she had taken over her year in Nepal, to Helambu. After a half hour, a group of children in blue uniforms caught up with her, yelling a raucous, 'Hello, hullo, hallow, hollow,' as they scampered past. A skinny boy tugged at her sweatshirt, grinning. In one breath, they both greeted each other with, 'Namaste.' The boy giggled and ran ahead. When Sarah caught up with Keshab another half hour later, she saw the skinny boy with him, chatting. She wanted to listen in on their conversation; she was curious about where the children were going. But when Keshab saw her approach, he started to walk again.

After walking for more than an hour alone, Sarah turned a bend and suddenly came upon Keshab waiting for her at the base of a hill, next to a vine with plump passion-flower buds. With a broad smile he said, 'Now it is four hours going up, what the boy told me. And for the tourist woman, six.' He laughed and patted the grass beside him, inviting her to sit.

'The tourist woman.' She flopped down beside him and took off her pack. Her shoulders were aching, as was the small of her back.

Keshab stared gravely at her cheeks. 'Your face is so red.'

'It always gets like that when I'm hot,' she said. She pulled out a bottle of mineral water. 'Want some?'

'I grew up drinking whatever tap, river water and never get sick.' Keshab gathered his pack. 'Let us go now.'

'Naai.' She put a hand on his pack to stop him from standing up. 'Let's rest awhile.'

Keshab obliged. He reached into a tangle of raspberry bushes behind her and plucked a few berries. 'Ainselu,' he said, placing them in her hands.

'Aiselu.'

'You eat.'

When the berries burst sweetly in her mouth, Sarah remembered that it was her birthday.

The next time she remembered that it was her birthday was forty minutes uphill, when she again came upon Keshab waiting for her. He pointed at a flowering camellia tree. 'We have in my village also. Chiniya gurans, means Chinese rhododendron.'

'They're beautiful,' she said, putting down her pack. The sight of the fleshy camellia blossoms cheered her a bit, though she had been feeling somewhat out of sorts since remembering that it was her birthday. She wondered if she should remind Keshab about it. Would that be too—childish?

'Walk with me,' she said instead. Again, he complied. He let her lead as they climbed a steep row of steps. Every now and then he would point out other plants that he knew from his childhood village: sycamore and walnut trees, alder and ash and yew. 'Such jungle we have in my home also,' he said as they entered a rhododendron forest. Pointing at a mulberry bush, he said, 'This one goats like. Silkworms also.' He placed his hands on Sarah's back and pushed her up a particularly steep stretch through the forest.

In Ulleri village, the lodge they stopped at for lunch was perched on a hillside of barley fields, with windows facing north. 'The mountains are usually visible,' the lodge keeper said apologetically, showing them to a cheerfully decorated dining room. She was dressed in colourful Indonesian batiks. 'But today, it looks like rain.' She placed a jar of plastic flowers on their table, and dusty salt and pepper shakers. Then she asked Keshab, 'Which trekking company are you from?'

He bristled. 'I'm not a guide.'

'What kind of work brings you here, then?'

'We're just friends, walking.'

The lodge keeper blushed. 'Eh.'

The menu she gave them promised piza, pankake, fry egges, mash pototo. They ordered two Swiss rostis with double eggs, and two apple pies with custard.

After the lodge keeper went to the kitchen, Sarah said, 'I guess they think you're a trekking guide.'

'This is natural,' Keshab said, and quickly followed with, 'Do you like to go to Ghorepani tonight?'

The weight of the pack had Sarah's shoulders throbbing, and the soles of her feet were tender. But it was only ten to one now. She nodded. 'Jaaney.'

'Djaaney.' He said, 'You American girl with so strong bones. All that hamburger you are eating as child. You must walk faster than me.'

The meal reinvigorated them, and after lunch they walked steadily—together—till it started to drizzle. They stopped on a ridge with a lone tea shop, sheltering in its thatched awning. Sarah put on her parka and Keshab his windbreaker, and then they headed up the path into the forest, which was thick, in this patch, with rhododendron trees. The balls of Sarah's feet began to hurt quite badly. She fell behind, though Keshab too was walking quite slowly by now. The only things she could hear were their footsteps and the pattering rain. Sometimes a drop would filter through the trees and plop on to her face, surprising her.

After several hours, they reached Ghorepani. It was late in the afternoon. Resting on their lodge's front steps, Sarah looked out at the green-brown rhododendron leaves catching the evening light, shimmering against the rain-soaked hills. She picked up a leaf that had fallen at her foot. Its midrib was mustard yellow. She again remembered that it was her birthday. She twirled the leaf in her hands. At thirty, this was where she was.

The next day Sarah's feet hurt so badly that she could barely walk out of the bedroom to the lodge's dining room. When she did, she found Keshab sitting by the window looking on to a horizon of silver clouds. 'There,' he said with a triumphant tone that struck her as curious. 'Annapurna is blocked by clouds.' He pointed at a blue streak in the clouds where the mountain peaks should have been.

They had a breakfast of oatmeal porridge. Keshab paid again, and then they began to walk. Sarah's shins shot with pain at each step. Past a police station, the muddy trail led downhill, forcing her to place all her weight on the soles of her feet. She was hobbling, like an old lady.

Keshab was quite unaffected by the earlier day's walk. Every now and then he even tried to rush her. 'I've got shin splints,' she would plead. He would cluck in exasperation. She did not understand his impatience. He seemed embarrassed when a group of Japanese trekkers overtook them, each member turning to nod their greetings to them. They were using ski poles as walking sticks. Behind them their Nepali porters skipped along, their rubber slippers slapping the trail.

Soon, Keshab left her, and began walking ahead. Was this insensitivity? Or was it something cultural—to walk alone? Today, this irritated Sarah, who stopped time and again to see if

Keshab would come back to find her. No: he would just wait for her, and when she caught up he would exhort her, 'You must walk faster,' and take off again. Surely he knew she would want his company as she walked. What was going on, she wondered. Was he embarrassed to be seen with her, afraid of being thought her trekking guide?

In the late morning, Sarah came upon a slab of slate rock that—once she sat down on—she seemed incapable of getting off. She shoved off her pack and massaged her sore neck. Around her, everything was silent. The mountains were still under cloud cover. The wheat fields were thinner than they had been lower south. A house in the distance was quiet and abandoned. Why was everything so still? She wondered: Where are the people? Were they working in the fields? Or was the village just empty? If Keshab were here he could explain. Such details would be full of significance in his presence.

She suddenly heard footsteps and turned to see Keshab marching towards her. 'Cow,' he yelled, and grabbed her pack, pulling her off the rock just as a large herd of cows appeared from a bend in the path. The animals lumbered past, veering all over the trail. Their minder, a mere boy, skipped up to them and asked in broken English what time it was. 'Twelve,' Keshab said. In English he said to Sarah, 'We stop at one for lunch.' Then he handed her her pack and started to walk off.

Rattled for no real reason, Sarah decided to talk to him at lunch, and ask him to walk with her. But an hour later, sitting in a wayside restaurant with a bowl of thukpa noodles in her hands, she found herself capable only of appreciating the immediate comfort of being able to rest and nourish herself. In any case Keshab was with her now, asking how bad the pain in her legs was. Had it been simply for such attentions—the companionship he offered as she made her way through an unfamiliar land—that she had fallen in love with him? Had it been because she had needed a translator, a guide? Sometimes she couldn't trust her own motivations.

He said, 'We can stay in this lodge today if it must be.'

Strengthened by the thukpa noodles and unwilling to own up to her frailty, Sarah said she would rather walk.

That afternoon it drizzled again. Drenched, and cursing her luck, Sarah trudged on, coaxing herself out of the urge to sit on every flat rock she passed. Every now and then she saw Keshab, far ahead, fleeting through rows of rain-darkened shrubs. It was only towards four, when she reached the top of the steps to Tatopani village, that she finally lost heart. Her shins felt shattered and she was trembling from the day's effort. The rain had by now seeped through her hair and was trickling coldly over her face. Her feet were soaked in her boots. The hills around were speckled with houses. There was no movement in any of their windows. Where were all the people? Where was Keshab? She felt utterly alone. To her own dismay, she began to cry.

After a long time Keshab came back to her, carrying a crooked ash branch. She had stopped crying by then. Now she was angry.

'What the fuck, Keshab,' she hissed as he sat down beside her. 'You keep walking ahead. You're leaving me all alone here. Fuck! I don't like it. I really don't!'

Gravely, he said, 'Do not use bad words, Saa'rah.'

'Fuck!' She sputtered again, 'Fuck!'

He set to whittling the ash branch into a walking stick. 'Now you will go faster,' he said finally, placing the stick in her hands.

He helped her up and guided her across a wet, mossy plank that served as a bridge over a steep gully. She held on to his hand as they walked further on the trail. To distract her, he declared, 'We take Nepali lesson now. Chiplo.' He pointed at the path ahead. 'Means slippy.'

Sarah smiled, feeling like a child. 'Slippery,' she said. 'Not slippy.'

'Repeat: Yo baato chiplo tcha.'

She gave in and repeated this sentence, as well as the other sentences he intoned for her: it is cold today; this is the way; you are walking too fast; I am using a stick. These weren't the topics she would rather have talked about: 'Mero khutta dukhyo.' My feet hurt. Don't go there. Look at that rhododendron. It will stop raining soon.

Still, the distraction was helpful. When they reached Tatopani village, they found most of the lodges full, crowded with damp-haired, scruffy Europeans looking delighted with life.

At the far end of the settlement, an old man finally offered them a room in his lodge. The room was dark, with a narrow space between the two single beds. Sarah immediately struggled out of her wet sweatshirt and pants and crawled naked into the covers. There she lay, giddy and numb, her ears ringing with exhaustion. The covers were dirty. She prayed they didn't have lice. At one point she looked around blearily, and realized that Keshab was no longer in the room. What the fuck was he up to? She was helpless to do anything but feel her body tingle with relief as it warmed.

After what seemed like forever, Keshab showed up with a quarter bottle of Challenger Whisky and two glasses of hot water. He poured them a drink each, gulped down his glass, and said, 'Medicine.'

'I'm going to die,' Sarah groaned. But she forced herself up, downed her whisky, then waited for the rush of alcohol to hit.

Keshab repeated, 'Now you must go to the hot spring.'

'I can't.'

'You must.'

Grudgingly, Sarah slipped on a T-shirt and shorts, and followed him, feeling dazed, out through the village lane. The spring was beyond the village, a pool carved into a river shore. Some foreigners were soaking themselves there, their pale, pink shoulders gleaming in the steaming water. There were also some Nepali men in the pool, but no local women. Sarah stepped into the water, then glided deeper into the heat, immediately eased.

That night she dreamed that she was walking downhill, on loose scree. She awoke with a start when she lost her footing.

She woke to less pain the next morning. Her legs still hurt, but they weren't tearing in pain. She felt less fragile as they walked, after breakfast, into cooler, higher altitudes. The air was dry here. The sky was clear today, but now some foothills were blocking the view of the Annapurna range.

Today, Keshab seemed to want to walk together. Why this change? Sarah couldn't guess. 'Now you can see education system in grass-root level,' he said as they entered a high pine forest. 'In your office you write all the reports about how much your American aid money has improved the education sector of

Tilled Earth

Nepal, but now you see the reality. No one lodge keeper we meet has studied in school.'

'I know what the education sector is like,' Sarah said. 'That's what I'm paid to know, remember?'

Keshab smiled. 'That is the thing.'

Then he launched into tales of his childhood, describing the friends with whom he swam in the rivers and stole fruit, the overly strict headmasters they played pranks on and the rules that barred Dalit students from entering the classrooms or sharing tap water. Sarah had heard some of these stories before, but she enjoyed hearing them again. She wondered at how utterly inscrutable his childhood was. He was so familiar to her, and yet, at the same time, so foreign. What she liked most about him was his sweet disposition. She trusted him instinctively. He had a life quite apart from her, she knew: a very Nepali life that she could not enter, and did not really want to. She hardly knew what that life was like. Yet she also knew him, deeply. Once, at the American club in Kathmandu, which she visited for weekly burgers-and-fries, an expat had warned her about the insidious methods Nepalis used to seduce American women. 'They'll use any means to get a visa,' the woman had sneered. Sarah had wondered if the woman had known about Keshab and her. Her superior tone had repelled Sarah. Her entire attitude had. Us and them. The rich and the poor. The white woman and the brown man. The highly paid consultant and the poorly paid language teacher.

It had only made Sarah try harder to open her heart to Keshab. And in any case, what could she offer him that he couldn't find in Nepali women? It wasn't as if they were planning to marry so that he could go to America. Of course one could never be sure; but as far as Sarah could tell, Keshab no more wanted to go to America than she wanted to live all her life here.

Actually, Keshab's mild, gentle manners rarely hinted at what he was thinking.

'Salla,' he now said when they sat down to rest. He was pointing at the forest around them.

She said, 'Pine.'

He pointed at a patch of grass.

'Ghaans,' she said. 'I know that one.' She pointed at a creeper with small red berries.

'Sarpe kaaphal. It is poison, you will die.'

'It looks like strawberry'

He held up his thumb. 'Strawberry is red, this size? It is sour? I ate once at five-star hotel seminar.'

Thankfully it didn't rain all day. They reached a small village, had a lunch of potato pancakes and, after Keshab paid, they walked together, chatting amiably. Sarah talked about her brother's struggle to recover from spinal injury. He had had an accident that had left him wheelchair-bound. She had deferred her arrival in Nepal by a year because of this. Keshab, in turn, talked about his mother's death when he was fourteen years old. He had taken her to Patna for treatment, but it had been futile. The words he used to express his loss were, 'I felt who is there left in my world.'

They reached Lete village at dusk and went to the first lodge on the path. A teenage boy there asked, 'One room or two?'

Sarah didn't catch Keshab's reply. The boy led them up a

flight of wooden stairs. When they reached the top, Keshab said, 'One.'

The attendant showed them to a room with flimsy wood walls. Sarah wouldn't have thought more about it, but once in the room, Keshab looked serious. 'People will be knowing me soon,' he said as they put down their packs. 'Two days from district headquarters, they will be recognizing me.'

Sarah was surprised by how much this hurt her. 'We could take separate rooms,' she said, wishing she could sound like it didn't matter.

'Tomorrow,' he said, avoiding her eyes. 'We must.'

We must. It was unreasonable of her to resent this, she knew. Keshab lived by the rules of his society, and had to keep up appearances. He was too caught up in Nepali mores to be truly free. He could not be seen to be sleeping with an American woman. Which was only part of all that was askew in their relationship. Perhaps dinner was the right time to talk, Sarah thought, to establish the fact that their relationship was going to end when she left Nepal.

They put on warm sweaters and went down to the dining room. There were three American men at a large table. Sarah was about to sit at another table, but one of the men called out, 'It's warmer here,' and Keshab went and sat down with them. Sarah followed reluctantly. There was a coal fire underneath the table. Its warmth was trapped by a heavy wool tablecloth covering everyone's legs.

One of the men was very attractive, with thick, black lashes that set off his pale blue eyes. He nodded at Sarah, and she nodded back. He and his friends were all wearing stylish, branded mountain gear, and they had a healthy, boyish air about them.

'Daal-bhat?' the teenage boy who seemed to run the lodge asked Keshab, adding, 'It's the only thing we serve.'

'And a quarter bottle of vodka,' he said.

'Yeah, so my grandfather,' the pale-eyed man said, continuing a conversation that they had interrupted. He caught Sarah's eyes, including her in the conversation. 'My grandfather thinks we should have stayed on in Vietnam.'

The other men laughed. One said, 'You know, my granddad's so old he calls them gooks. It's not that he's racist,' he insisted. 'It's just that whole generation, you know, thinks the rest of the world's full of shit.'

The pale-eyed man caught Sarah's eyes again.

The third man mentioned that his grandfather had served in the first Iraq war.

Then the conversation veered elsewhere. The pale-eyed man revealed that he worked as a scuba instructor in St. Lucia. The other two were from Minnesota. They had apparently met up on the trail, today, and had decided to walk together from tomorrow. Sarah wondered why they were all talking so loudly.

She turned to Keshab, and, in an attempt to have their own conversation, she said, 'That hot spring was great yesterday.'

Keshab did not reply. He was going through the quarter bottle of vodka quite rapidly. He was obviously interested in what the other men were saying; he kept trying to catch their eyes so he could join in. Sarah caught the scuba instructor looking at him, then at her. She quickly looked away.

Finally the scuba instructor turned to Keshab. 'You guys trekking?'

'We are from Kathmandu,' Keshab declared, with the loud

tone he had when he was drunk. 'I am from Nepal. I am novelist.'

The man's eyes slid from him to Sarah.

'And I work in Kathmandu,' she explained. She disliked him for no real reason. An awkward silence set in.

Then the man with the racist grandfather started up about ice hockey, a game he had always dug. Everyone turned to him.

Keshab listened on keenly. When the men started to talk about their porters, he finally broke in, 'There is great exploitation.'

The men turned to him, and he continued, 'There is no minimum wage rate for the porters in Nepal.'

The scuba instructor said, 'Really?'

'It is a fact.'

The scuba instructor smiled politely. Then the others returned to talking about their grandfathers.

Keshab noticed the rebuff, and withdrew. Sarah felt weirdly avenged. Not all Americans are like me, she wanted to say to him. Not all Americans make an effort to reach out. Especially to—a novelist. A socialist. She felt angry at the men for not extending themselves. She placed her hand on Keshab's thigh, feeling protective.

That night, curled against Keshab's back, Sarah listened to the distant sound of the men's chatter in the dining room, to the rolling cadences of fast-spoken American English. This was the first time she had ever lived abroad. Had she changed? She tried to remember if she had ever spoken like these men, so lively and jangling about nothing.

The next day, an hour from Lete, a cold sleet whipped down from the sky. They were walking along the dry shores of the

Kali Gandaki River, in a spare brown canyon speckled with juniper trees. Sarah stopped to put on her parka. Keshab poked around in his pack and said he couldn't find his windbreaker. 'I left it somewhere I think.'

'You lost it?' Sarah was irritated by this. 'People suffer needlessly because they are careless.' She did not feel like she could wear her parka if Keshab was going to be freezing. She took it off and insisted he wear it. He refused. Frustrated, she cried, 'Well I'm not going to,' and thrust it into his hands and strode off in a huff.

Her legs had recovered by now, and were feeling toned. Fuelled by a sudden burst of energy, she walked so fast that she soon left Keshab behind. Along the river shores the wind eddied around her, tossing up sand. The sleet prickled against her arms. The colder it grew the faster Sarah walked, just to keep her body warm. She clenched her fists to keep her fingers from freezing.

The mountains were finally visible today. But the Annapurna range was out of sight by now. The Nilgiri range loomed to the right, and to the left, stolid Dhaulagiri. It was too frigid to stop and admire the view, though. The jagged blue ice on the mountains was quite ethereal, but Sarah just wanted to reach the shelter of a lodge.

There were very few people on the trail today. In the late morning, she spotted a dark figure far ahead of her. Maybe it was the scuba instructor from last night. The prospect of meeting him now seemed to please her. St. Lucia. She had always wanted to go to the Caribbean on vacation. Perhaps if her brother recovered enough, they could go together... As she neared the figure, though, she saw it was a man dressed in flimsy cotton loincloths. A Hindu ascetic. The ascetic's back, thin and bony, was entirely exposed. He was walking with a limp, with one foot dragging on the path. Passing him, Sarah saw that the dragging foot was a plastic prosthesis.

She suddenly felt lost. She stopped where she was, allowing the ascetic to overtake her as she waited for Keshab to catch up with her.

When he did, he surprised her by kissing her. 'You wear,' he said, placing the parka on her shoulders. 'Do not act like little child.'

They walked together from there, soon catching up with the ascetic. He said something to Keshab, and Keshab said something back. The ascetic's matted hair gave him a wild, animal look. Sarah wondered if he was cold. Should she offer her parka to him? Or would that be ridiculous? Maybe the ascetic didn't feel any bodily pain.

Keshab turned to her. 'Saa'rah, I must see the map.'

From her pack, she took out the Department of Roads and Transportation map that she had borrowed from a colleague in Kathmandu. Squatting on the ground, Keshab spread the map over the trail. The ascetic bent over and placed a finger on the village of Jomsom.

'No, we're here,' Keshab said in Nepali, pointing further down.

The two men consulted awhile, tracing the contours of the map.

Sarah felt self-conscious standing there, so she continued ahead. Keshab caught up with her in twenty minutes. He was now wearing his windbreaker. 'It was in my bag,' he said. 'When I put in the map, there it is. I found.'

Sarah's anger flared up. Didn't it mean anything to him that she had spent the morning so cold? Was he completely thoughtless? She didn't say anything to him, though. Her anger took on a cool, hard quality, and she almost enjoyed its hardness, its cold.

It was only when they reached a lodge in Tukuche village that she decided to put her anger aside. Perhaps this was because of a spongy chocolate cake that she and Keshab decided to share, the slice topped with a thick, fatty layer of cream. She asked Keshab about the ascetic. He had come from Benares on a pilgrimage to the Muktinath temple, considered holy by Hindus. 'How cold he must be,' Keshab said, and Sarah found herself arguing, 'But he wants to renounce bodily comfort, right? He wants to suffer. Right?'

Then Keshab told her that Tukuche village was the birthplace of one of Nepal's greatest poets, and Sarah found herself glazing over.

That evening, at their hotel in Marpha, Keshab asked for separate rooms.

Feeling defeated, Sarah followed the woman of the lodge to a second-floor room that looked on to green corn fields. She changed into the only clean outfit she had remaining. Downstairs, in the dining hall, Keshab was at a table, reading. A naked bulb hung above him, casting a warm pool of light on to him. Sarah settled across from him, making sure not to touch, or look improper. The dining room was decorated with posters of Thai landscapes. The benches and chairs were covered with Tibetan rugs. This was the nicest lodge they had stayed in yet. She wished they could have a few days here, just to themselves. But of course that would be impossible...

Over a hot rum punch, Keshab talked a little about the book he was reading, a collection of poems by a young writer from the district. 'It is about the village life. He writes on how much beauty in the life of rural farming. But also how difficult. He is member of communist party, not Maoist, but Marxist-Leninist. He is living in district headquarters, so I must read in case we meet tomorrow.' He laughed, and turned back to the book.

Sarah reached for a map of the trekking circuit, printed on the back of the lodge's menu. Birethanti, Ghorepani, Ghara, Kalopani, Tukuche, Marpha: black dots linked together by the crosshatch of a trail. She asked, 'What do you think we should do, then?'

Keshab didn't say anything.

'I booked my tickets last week.'

Keshab looked up from the book of poems. 'Lufthansa or Thai?'

She answered his question—'Lufthansa'—then turned to the window to look at the Nilgiri range. In the night, the mountain was a glimmer of blue. She felt an odd mix of emotions. She had expected, she now realized, for Keshab to kick up a fuss, insist that they remain together, and maybe even marry, so that he could go to America. She felt ashamed at this realization, but also disappointed that he had not kicked up a fuss. And somewhere at the back of her heart, she also felt relieved.

'The novel I write next,' Keshab said as they left Marpha the next morning, ambling now because they had only a few hours' walk left to the district headquarters, from where they were due to fly out the following day. 'That novel maybe I set in tourist lodge. Young boy is running hotel and falling in love with Japanese tourist lady. What do you think?'

Sarah laughed. 'Do they get married and go to Japan? Does he become a capitalist robot or will she live in the village and become a good Nepali girl?'

'It is tragedy,' Keshab said, smiling broadly. He prided himself on never having written a love story. 'She goes back and he stays, but lucky thing, both people they become member of socialist party in their country, and they spend productive life fighting for worldwide exploited workers.'

'That sounds like a terrible novel.'

'Your leg it is no more hurting?'

'No.'

The Nilgiri range was now behind them, just south. The mountain tops were covered by clouds, and only the rocky mass of their base was visible. Sarah took pleasure in the slow pace of their walk today. She knew that she would lose Keshab when they reached the district headquarters, Jomsom. There would be local writers and intellectuals there, people he would want to meet, talk to, pay his respects to. He was too well known to remain hers there.

In fact, she lost Keshab even before they reached Jomsom. He fell into conversation with another man on the trail, and it turned out the man knew the poet whose book he had been reading the night before. The two men began to talk in high, literary Nepali, and Sarah could only catch a bit of what they were saying: 'You must come to my house,' 'Are plane tickets easy to come by?' 'Does the chairman know you're coming?'

She followed behind, giving in to her own silence. This silence she was used to. This silence was part of her relationship with Keshab. It was part of all that was said between them, these silences that bred misunderstanding, but also trust, sympathy and love.

When they reached Jomsom, Keshab introduced her to the man he'd met with a cryptic: 'My colleague at the office.'

They took their leave of the man, and chose a lodge owned by a cousin of the poet. Then Keshab left her to fix their tickets, and to visit acquaintances.

Sitting in the sun tanning herself, Sarah found herself feeling all right. There was really nothing much to talk about with Keshab in the end. She would leave. He would stay. Their affinity wouldn't translate through letters, faxes, telephone calls. She realized: talking about that wouldn't make it not happen. It would just make things more painful. That was probably why Keshab had avoided the topic entirely. That was why he had not said, on this trek, what he once used to say to her all the time: Timi mero saa'rah sansar hau. You are my entire world.

The view of the Niligiri range was completely blocked by clouds that afternoon. To allay a sadness that was creeping up on her, Sarah turned her mind to other matters. The money she had given Keshab to cover her expenses must have long since run out, she thought. Throughout, they had eaten daal-bhat dinners for seventy-five rupees a meal. She took out a notebook and did the math. When they had stopped for tea they had often had glucose biscuits as well. At one lodge—she forgot where—they had shared a chocolate cake. In one lodge they had had hot rum punch. For lunch they had usually eaten Swiss rosti with fried eggs: sixty rupees. She had ordered cheese omelettes every breakfast, and he had ordered Tibetan bread: forty-five rupees each.

When Keshab returned in the late afternoon, the two of them went for a short stroll through the town. They were careful not to walk too close, to keep up appearances. They did not say much, but they were content. At a small bookstore crammed with romances and thrillers, she bought him a *Newsweek*. For her he bought a Mars bar.

'Bholi djaane?' Keshab asked at one point. *Are we going tomorrow?*

'Djaane,' she said, realizing that though in the years to come she might well speak the Nepali language with others, he was the only person with whom she would share its intimate silences.

Nineteen Years His Junior

~

First Urmila pruned the lemon bush on the balcony, cutting off all its crisp dead leaves with a pair of old scissors gone to rust. Then she untangled the jasmine vine from the iron grills that they had grown on to and propped up the stems, making sure they covered the water spots along the wall. Next she plucked the dry leaves off the jade plants that lined the balcony railing. What else needed doing in this flat free of parents-in-law and family members? She was a liberated woman: she used to be active in district politics. Now here she was in Kathmandu. The sky was darkening rapidly. She had to squint to see. She started to snap off the dead shoots of the bamboo plant but she could not tell apart the dead from the live shoots, so she took up a broom and began to sweep the balcony floor. When she tasted dust in her mouth she realized all she was doing was raising a dust storm. So she put down the broom and fetched a bucketful of water from inside. She sprinkled liberal handfuls of water into the indigo night. Then she felt about for the rusty scissors, crouching in the dark till she found them on the floor. By the time she found them it was nine, and she was tired and no longer agitated that dinner had long since cooled again, tonight, exactly a year after her marriage to the party's central committee member nineteen years her senior.

41

The Secretary of the Student Union Makes a Career Choice

~

Ramesh had left the hostel to buy a backup battery so he could work on the computer even when the lights went out, but he had come back with a bag of fresh vegetables. It seemed to indicate to him that he wasn't sure what to do in life. It was true: sometimes he thought he should work in the software industry; other times he thought he wanted to be an actor. He didn't know anyone in the cinema industry who could get him a role. One needed the right connections. He was just the secretary of the student union. Night-times he slept hard, and daytimes he wandered, looked, looked at newspapers, read, read the headlines, and talked to people about toppling the government. But it was other professions he dreamed of. Sometimes he thought he wanted to learn how the wind turned blades, how water turned turbines, how the heat of the sun got trapped in black metal pipes. He often thought of quitting computer science and enrolling in the engineering campus. He also liked nature and believed in stopping global warming. Sometimes he felt he could spend his life walking high trans-Himalayan trails looking at blue sheep through powerful binoculars, spotting endangered

42

animals and rare plants and saving them from extinction. There were so many urgent callings. One night in bed he heard a BBC radio interview of a woman who walked in the dark focusing on the ground in order to improve her night vision. He should learn how to do that, he thought. Or he should write. He could write a novel. Why not? He should write a novel about his distant aunt, spit foaming the sides of her mouth, and write again, and rewrite, revise. Why not paint, though? It was important to live a full life, a life coloured by the imagination. 'Your problem,' his mother had said to him once, 'is that you have too many talents.' She just wanted him to find work after completing his studies. But he wanted a life of freedom. Why could he not teach yoga or meditation for a living? Om shanti shanti om. He could teach tourists how to focus on the pauses in the ins and outs of the breath. Yes. No. One had to be practical. His mother, father, sisters were counting on him. So? He could become an engineer, but a special kind of engineer, an engineer with a mission. He would build culverts, bridges and irrigation canals in far-flung districts. There were many villages that needed development. When he thought of villages, though, he also thought: he could become an anthropologist, study the ways of remote tribes. He could fall in love with foreign women who came on academic grants. He had always been good with people. He could even become a psychiatrist. He knew how to counsel the distressed. Recently a friend of his had married a woman he didn't love, and had talked to him for hours at the hostel, about the waves of fear that now washed over him. 'I can't go anywhere without feeling terrified,' his friend had said. 'I feel like everything's going wrong. I'm afraid all the time.'

Fear, Ramesh had thought. He should alleviate the insecurity gnawing at people. He had reached over, wanting to take his friend's hand in his, wanting to give him some succour. But hearing a newspaper vendor outside the hostel window shouting aloud the news that the government had been overturned, he had dropped his friend's hand, and run out to politick.

Tilled Earth

Friends

~

By day, Kathmandu's tourist district Thamel hawks trinkets and
curios. The Dutch, the Italian, the German, the Japanese, the
French, the American, the Israeli—tourists, all—come to the
memorabilia shops here to buy Buddhist mandalas, turquoise
bracelets, Gurkha knives, bottled water, pashmina shawls, demon
masks, rice-paper notebooks, chocolate bars, hiking boots,
embroidered T-shirts that read I Love Mount Everest. A roll of
Fuji film sells for three hundred here, and twenty rupees less
over there; each price is negotiable. All day the streets bustle
with bargaining: 'Sixty.' 'Last price fifty.' As evening falls,
Thamel crowds travellers into its low-budget restaurants, and
turns them wide-eyed with wonder because serendipity has
brought them together in—of all places—Kathmandu, Nepal.
'Life is so wonderful.' For under two dollars each, they can eat
eggplant lasagne, garlic naan, schnitzel, swimming rama, stir-
fries, buffalo dumplings, risotto, curry or pizza, and swap
adventures and world views. 'My meditation teacher said flowers
bloom even in the desert.' 'I found an awesome used bookstore
selling Pico Iyer.' 'The first main thing I don't like of Nepal,'
tourists declare in broken English, 'is the dirty air.' Indeed, the

exhaust from the city's cars and buses is one of the largest cracks in this patchy, fogged mirror image of western dreams—a mirror quicksilvered with tall mountain stories, some fantastic tales of Kew and a Cat Stevens song about Kathmandu.

The more traditional Nepalis who inhabit Thamel, however, cannot begin to identify the syncopated beat of Bob Marley drowned by the wail of Joan Baez as they turn a corner. Hoping to profit from the neighbourhood's tourist bent, most of the locals have rented out their houses to hotels, restaurants and shops, moving their families to quieter neighbourhoods. The proper circles of Kathmandu even shun Thamel. Driving by on some rare occasion, the nation's who's who murmur, 'This is where we used to play ball as boys. It was just an empty field.' They exclaim, 'There was a sweetmeat store—and look, there it is, still, beneath that sign for International Trunk Call Fax Photocopy Services. I wonder if it's still run by that pock-marked shopkeeper.'

The sweetmeat store, as it happens, has changed hands several times, and now belongs to Kuber Sharma, a recent migrant from the south, who takes the growth of concrete houses around his shop as a personal insult. 'Why can't *I* have a house of my own?' he mutters at a picture of Laxmi, the goddess of wealth, as he heats the oil in which he fries, for one despondent hour every morning, the crisp sugared sweetmeats that he will sell for the rest of the day. Warding off flies, sipping weak tea, counting change for customers, Kuber Sharma curses his fate and his young wife——who makes expensive demands of him, but he does, at the end of each month, make enough to meet his rent and living costs.

Tenzing Namgyal in the art store next door doesn't believe in god because Tenzing is Tibetan, and the Buddha said there is no god. Tenzing is flexible, though, and he will question his views when talking to foreign women. The prettier the foreign women are, the more god-fearing Tenzing is inclined to become. 'This is Avalokitesvara, future Buddha,' he says in his high-school English, spreading for her benefit a scrolled acrylic painting. 'One hundred per cent vegetable dye.' He fingers the deity's pink navel. 'For you only two thousand. Where you from, Italian?'

Kamal Malla, a young computer programmer, strolls by Tenzing's store every evening on his way back from work. He is charmed by this part of the city, so different from his own staid, duty-bound parts of Kathmandu. When the sky darkens and halogen lights switch on of their own accord, he hears old men and women greet each other anew, as per custom, as though a new day has begun, and indeed it always seems to have. Rust-coloured lights warm the air. Pedlars press close and whisper, 'Hashish?' 'Tiger balm?' 'Change money?' Irate tourists brush them off: 'No, no, no.' Flutes and saxophones riddle the night. Kamal stops to take in picturesque sights: a white man with a long, pierced nose. Fantastic! They stretch the imagination, the things he sees here. And so each day after work, he ambles along in the vicinity of—one block away from, one storey down from, one door over from, one street up from—Thamel dwellers like Dilip Basnyat, the owner of La Vie Boheme Restaurant, who worries about his skinny cook, who makes an exquisite borscht soup but disappears for days, explaining, when he returns, that he had to consult his village witch doctor about an illness that won't go away: 'I lose weight no matter how much I eat.' Of course Kamal Malla doesn't know Dilip Basnyat; he has never been inside La Vie Boheme. Such restaurants are for tourists. Yet it affects him, the vivid, juddering tensions of the neighbourhood at night. It's as if he becomes more vigilant, less placid, a bit unfamiliar to himself. Volatile, changeable, edgy. Like the waiter at the Third World European Cuisine, Lal Bahadur Rai, who keeps a lookout for single foreign men to ask them if they want a nice Nepali girl—hoping to marry his sister, at sixteen, to a kind and gentle foreigner, preferably a Britisher, because they are civilized. In Thamel, Kamal awakens from his traditional life and becomes just a little more modern; I can see this from the open, interested expression on his face as he passes by my small but well-located convenience store.

On one of his evening walks last year, Kamal came across Hrishikesh Pandey, a Nepali who had recently returned from the United States where he had lived since childhood. Hrishikesh saw Kamal first, actually, and recognized him by his white shirt with candy stripes, which Kamal wore almost every day. 'It's you,' Hrishikesh said, reaching out to get the other man's attention.

Kamal had been inspecting a display of peach strudels, and was startled. 'Eh.' He turned and smiled politely, unable to place the lean, lanky boy smiling down at him so familiarly. The boy spoke Nepali but wore tourist rags, and was as pale as a foreigner.

Hrishikesh asked, 'Do you live around here?' He leaned into Kamal as a man swept by hissing, 'Hashish?'

'Yes, I remember,' Kamal said, suddenly brightening up. 'Your Pentium—Toshiba, I think, yes, now I'm sure. Laptop.' Then he stopped smiling. 'I've been meaning to telephone you.'

'Hey, no problem.'

Hrishikesh asked which way Kamal was heading, and the two of them walked together into the crowded centre of Thamel, past my shop, towards a row of carpet vendors, halting every time a bicycle or battered taxi swerved too close. Kamal talked about the computer. 'You need a new motherboard,' he said, trying to remember all the details. He mentioned a friend's shop, where prices were middling. 'I'll put it into the computer if you like.'

Hrishikesh had already looked into buying a PowerBook, and preferred, anyway, to set a more casual tone to their talk. Kamal had struck him as nice when they'd met at the Computer Centre. He watched Kamal pull out a pack of Khukuri filters and light one without offering him any. This seemed very Nepali to Hrishikesh, who studied other Nepalis in order to learn about himself. Despite the smart office clothes that Kamal wore, he looked utterly native, with his jet-black hair, ashen skin, elongated eyes and sharp nose. He had the chiselled brown lips of a cast-iron Buddha.

'There's a nice garden restaurant here,' Hrishikesh said, stopping in front of La Vie Boheme Restaurant. 'Can I buy you a beer?'

Kamal hesitated, but he was too polite to refuse. But he worried, as soon as they took a table, about his sister at home, who would be cooking dinner for him. While Hrishikesh ordered beer—'San Miguel, not Iceberg'—and snacks—'Do you have chips? And that borscht soup?'—Kamal wondered if he should call home and say he'd be late but the waiter moved away and there was this boy Hrishikesh, reclined on a cane chair, his unkempt hair falling on to his forehead, shading his wide-set, friendly eyes.

Without any prompting, Hrishikesh began to talk about himself, explaining that it had been just a few months since he had come to Nepal. 'I wanted to find out who I really am,' he said, and his frank tone intrigued Kamal. Apparently, he was staying with his uncle—'But I don't think family is as important as friends'—and he was a journalist, working for the *Kathmandu Newsflash*. Kamal noted that Hrishikesh spoke Nepali with a child's vocabulary, peppering it with many English words.

The beer and chips came, then the soup, and they shared everything, Kamal slowly drawn into Hrishikesh's curious banter. The boy seemed simple, like a child who couldn't contain what he felt, and had to blurt it out.

'I don't really know anything about my own country,' Hrishikesh admitted, looking flustered. Kamal noticed the redness of the boy's face, but didn't think much of it. He was enjoying this garden restaurant filled with tourists, with Billy Joel scratched over the speakers, singing praises of a girl from uptown. A naked bulb cast deep blue shadows on Hrishikesh's sunken face. 'I don't even know,' Hrishikesh continued, breaking into English, which he spoke more naturally than Nepali. 'I don't even know the difference between Pandeys and Mallas.'

The beer buzzed in Kamal's mind, and he decided to match Hrishikesh's frankness with his own. In English, he said. 'There is some differences in what festival your family is celebrating and my family. Small-small differences, I don't know. But all this is nothing about culture and religion. You have to be modern and don't look back.'

Hrishikesh lifted his glass of beer and toasted this. When he put down the glass he asked, still looking anxious, 'What language do you speak with your family?'

'Nepal-bhasa. Newari,' Kamal said, then laughed. 'You are probably speaking English at home. Nepali is both not our mother tongue.'

Both men eased into their chairs. They spent the next hour chatting about Kathmandu in vague, general terms, Hrishikesh asking questions, and Kamal outlining the city's various problems: poverty, pollution, politics. He wasn't saying anything that Hrishikesh hadn't heard before—all Nepalis seemed obsessed with poverty, pollution and politics. But still, it was fun listening to Kamal. There was something about the way he talked—with a soothing tone—that made Hrishikesh feel less alone than he had been feeling in this city. He hadn't actually been able to make any friends yet. And as for Kamal, he savoured the novelty of the experience, sitting in a restaurant like this, talking to a half-American boy who spoke so guilelessly, like a child. La Vie Boheme Restaurant—he must remember the name. The music—which band was it, it sounded familiar—and the soup, the cheap cane-and-cotton decor put him in a giddy, light-hearted mood.

Outside La Vie Boheme, Kamal lit up a cigarette. Hrishikesh asked for one too.

'It's a nice night,' Hrishikesh said after lighting up, still feeling chatty.

Kamal laughed, 'Only at night Kathmandu is beautiful,' and went off with a nod.

Alone in the cool, dark night, both men felt affirmed by their exchange.

R. P. Aryal, the editor-in-chief of the *Kathmandu Newsflash*, liked putting the Pandey boy down. He derived a sharp, tingly pleasure from it. 'The Cultural Attaché of the Bangladesh Embassy,' he would say, making the assignment sound important as he handed the attaché's calling card to Hrishikesh. 'We need some pictures of floods.' And off the boy would go, in his ugly German sandals, to fetch pictures like a peon. Radiant and sincere, Hrishikesh seemed to invite, even facilitate, his own degradation. He didn't know about office hierarchy, and he never asked for taxi money, perks or reimbursement for the cost of rikshaas. He paid all his expenses out of his meagre three-thousand-rupee salary. RP figured that the boy's father was rich—one earned millions in America—and liked the thought that Hrishikesh was returning that wealth back to Nepal. Yes. RP enjoyed this thought. To his friends who came to the office to drink tea and gossip away the afternoon, RP would say, 'Green-card holding pure Nepali boy, that one.' His friends would turn to look at Hrishikesh, dressed like a hippy in loose-fitting natural-fibre clothes. RP would add, 'Says he wants to live in Nepal, who knows for how long.'

And his friends would speculate.

Hrishikesh knew none of this, but felt a bit isolated in the *Kathmandu Newsflash* office, where he was the youngest staff member. He admired RP because the man knew everyone, but didn't really like him; there was something sinister about the way he looked at people, as if always appraising their worth.

Neither did he like the assistant editor, who didn't show Hrishikesh any of the camaraderie he displayed the rest of the staff. The staff themselves—perhaps because of their limited English and his limited Nepali—kept their distance from Hrishikesh. Most days Hrishikesh sat alone at his desk proofreading his colleagues' articles. Their grammar was so strangulated he had no choice but to rewrite whole paragraphs, sometimes whole articles. If he asked, he was also allowed to write his own articles, which made him feel that his life in Nepal had some purpose. The other journalists at the *Kathmandu Newsflash* noted, with some bitterness, that Hrishikesh Pandey's articles were grammatically correct but gratingly high-minded. They knew much more about deforestation, homeless children, hydro-power, sustainable development, urbanization; but they didn't have good English, that was all.

Hrishikesh blamed himself for each rebuff he suffered in his bid for friendship with his colleagues. Perhaps he didn't know how to behave, how to fit in, be like a real Nepali, he thought. At the end of each day he returned to his uncle's home feeling exhausted from his day's efforts. Not that he regretted returning to Nepal. Every day he saw so much and learned so much about this place that was his country—what was a green card, after all; he was still a Nepali citizen. Yes, he was glad he had come home—yes, why not call it home; but there was no denying that life in Nepal could be—that was to say—it definitely seemed, at times, like a struggle.

A week or ten days after their chance meeting in Thamel, Hrishikesh walked into Kamal's office at the Computer Centre, wondering, as he passed through the dusty halls, if his crumpled orange shirt and baggy pants made him look like a tourist. He found Kamal at his desk, tinkering with electrical wires. Kamal stood up, pleased to see him, and immediately produced a wedding invitation—his sister was getting married—with the name Risikes misspelled in English. 'Tea?' Kamal asked, and rang a tinny bell on his desk, which produced a peon at the door. He ordered two cups. 'Here is your Toshiba,' he said, picking it out of a pile of keyboards, wires and monitors at the side of his desk.

Hrishikesh took the computer and listened to the other man's slightly over-long description of what had happened to the motherboard. This wasn't what he'd come for. 'Do you have a cigarette?' he said when Kamal was finished. Kamal cocked his head, smiled and pulled out his pack of Khukuri filters, and both men smoked.

The tea came, weak and watery. Kamal had the peon offer a cup to Hrishikesh first, then he took his own cup and sipped it while Hrishikesh complained about his work. 'I get so tired,' Hrishikesh said, and his face suddenly seemed all bone and cartilage. 'I write my own articles, and edit everyone else's, but nobody ever says good job, nobody gives a shit.'

Kamal was at first put off by this expletive, then pleased by its novelty. He watched the younger man—who must be what: twenty-three at most—and felt moved by his pout, his flighty gestures, his indignation at the difficulties of life in Nepal. Kamal took the tone of an elder brother, a role he immediately liked: 'You don't know, Kathmandu's people are mean.'

'But why?' Hrishikesh cried. 'Why are they mean?'

'They are very devious, you do not know,' Kamal said. 'I have grown here all my life, and I have seen all what they do to each other with their small-small minds.'

'Small thoughts,' Hrishikesh sighed. Then he realized he'd gone on too long, and asked Kamal about his work. 'Is it like that for you, too?'

Kamal glanced at the door. 'It is all crap,' he said with a rasp that surprised himself. He lowered his voice. 'These government offices, are all crap. These small-small minded people, I almost go crazy. Junior staffs like me they make to repair equipment. And senior staffs and bosses attend training programmes and seminars abroad, all crap.'

'I don't know much about computers,' Hrishikesh said. 'Do you like working with them?'

'In Pakistan,' Kamal said, sitting forward, 'Madras, South India—so many countries, the software programme is major industry.' He got a bit flustered at this thought. 'Is highly specialized labour, and in this parts of the world it is cheaper for big-big companies to hire. We could do programming in Nepal, too, but the government is too unstable—who would like to invest money? Every six months a new government. If the government were stable we could start software industry. Software, it is challenging. But not this hardware repair crap. I get excited, even thinking…'

He was getting carried away. Kamal checked himself, sat back, and smiled. It wasn't good to get riled up like this.

Hrishikesh stood. He had an errand to run, and he thanked Kamal for looking at his laptop.

'No need for thanks,' Kamal insisted. Hrishikesh was a friend now, and didn't have to be so formal.

He reached over and took the boy's hand. Hrishikesh found this gesture very Nepali. He reached for his wallet, but Kamal said, vehemently, 'No, no, no payment,' and shooed him out of the room. This boy acted too American at times.

Alone again in his office, Kamal returned to his wires, but he was distracted by the ambitions which had simmered to a boil inside him. Four months ago he had applied for the master's in computer science programme at the Asian Institute of Technology, in Bangkok. It was March now: about time for their response.

All of this took place last spring, when my husband and I were selling clothes because tourists, it seemed, wore anything. Someone had designed clashing blue-and-red pants and the brightest, most tasteless patch skirts. But even these, tourists tried on, said, 'Cool,' and bought. Our store was full of these mad rags, and also stocked with sweaters, shirts, caps and socks, all made in Nepal. My husband and I had taken a loan, so we needed at least eight thousand a month to cover our interest, rent and food. I found two tailors, low-caste boys from our district—we're originally from Syangja, in the western hills—and they sat in the back of the shop, stitching cotton patches on to our clothes to make them look fashionable. Our store didn't do well, though, and sometimes it looked like we'd never be able to pay back our loans.

Dilip Basnyat, the owner of La Vie Boheme—he's the one who lent us the money, he's a moneylender from our district—was advising us to display our products better. 'I know a Kashmiri family migrated here, rented a space,' he would say each time we visited him. 'Not even as big as yours. But they spent thousands on spotlights, on a showcase for their window. A year later,' he'd make an expansive gesture, 'they're already building a house.'

It was like he didn't realize that we couldn't afford luxuries like spotlights.

'You don't need a good space,' he would say with the certainty of the well-to-do, 'if you know how to market your products.'

Then he would explain why he couldn't lower our interest rate, and dismiss us with a wave. On our way out my husband and I would stop by the kitchen to talk to my cousin, the restaurant's head cook. My cousin looked sicklier with each passing day. He had a terminal blood disease which Dilip Basnyat didn't know about. If he were to die suddenly, Dilip Basnyat would truly suffer, I thought. Because no one else in Kathmandu could make the borscht soup that his restaurant was renowned for.

In the days leading up to his sister's wedding, Kamal stopped coming to Thamel because there was too much to do at home. When he got back from work every day, he found his father and uncles and cousin brothers in the ground-floor rooms watching satellite TV, and making plans for a bakery that they were going to open, Kamal's mother, aunts and cousin sisters were in the second-floor bedrooms sorting cardamom, cinnamon, walnuts, coconuts and rock sugar for the wedding banquet. Kamal would go to the kitchen on the top floor, where his sister, at the stove, would motion for him to sit. 'Have tea,' she would say, and go through the familiar, intimate gestures of brewing tea. Then she would say, 'You must be hungry,' and turn her attention to the lentil patties she was frying for snacks.

Kamal would watch her face: so serene, all smooth surface. She was a perfect girl in every way. Since high school, she had stayed at home, bringing him tea in the morning, making his bed and ironing his clothes. At night, she cooked the family dinner. Now a Poland-educated civil engineer had asked the family for her hand in marriage. They had all urged her to accept. Was she happy with this decision? It was impossible to tell. 'Not much time left,' Kamal would sometimes remark, looking at her closely, trying to decipher the subtle blush his words would produce.

His own ambitions stirred in him like a storm as he drank the tea she prepared, as he wondered what it would be like—if he got an acceptance letter—when he told his family that he was leaving Kathmandu, going to Bangkok. He hadn't even told them that he had applied. If he went, would his parents feel abandoned by their only son? Would his sister accuse him of failing his duties? She, who had never failed in any of her duties as a girl—woman.

Hrishikesh attended Kamal's sister's wedding, but briefly, uncomfortable to be among so many people who looked like they actually belonged there. Kamal attended to him in the gracious way of Nepali hosts: urging him to eat more, drink more, stay longer. 'You've only just got here.' But that week, Hrishikesh's thoughts had been occupied by a chain of events set off by the letter he'd got from his girlfriend in Boston announcing that she needed her freedom. He had called Eliza and found out that she had gone back to the boyfriend she'd had before him. For several giddy days, Hrishikesh had felt all alone in this vast world. To allay his fears, he had slept with an American volunteer he met writing an article on the Peace Corps. Jessica was an opinionated thirty-two-year-old who felt that Nepali peasants would benefit by eliminating the country's upper classes; and Hrishikesh had realized, even as he had crept out of her lodge at dawn, that he had made a mistake. When he had told her so, he had fuelled her class antagonism. She had accused him of being a self-absorbed and indulgent man of privilege, the son of a millionaire (oh, yes, she had heard what Nepalis paid for migration papers), and not even a real Nepali, like the villagers of the hill district Khotang where the Peace Corps had posted her. Miserably, Hrishikesh had realized that he didn't even know where Khotang was. He had responded to his confusion by enrolling in yoga classes, for which he had seen an ad in Jessica's lodge. His next article for the *Kathmandu Newsflash* was about his yoga instructors, two brothers from North India who viewed bliss as a way of life. His article was titled 'Nepalis Must Expand Their Consciousness'.

Back at work in the Computer Centre, Kamal flipped absentmindedly through the *Kathmandu Newsflash* and wondered when the Asian Institute of Technology in Bangkok would send word of his acceptance.

A few weeks passed. My husband and I, in that period, realized we'd make more money if we sold things that people couldn't do without. We fired the tailor boys, shoved our stock of clothes to the back corner of the store, and set up a modest window display of plastic combs, Chinese soap, dandruff shampoo, sandalwood incense, playing cards, Nivea cold cream, Colgate toothpaste and Indian nail cutters. We added postcards and rice-paper calendars and prayer wheels to our stock, and also Nice biscuits. 'What shall I buy you, my little round love,' my husband would say, embracing me at night, 'with all the money we'll make?'

Now I'm not the kind of woman who needs jewellery, lipstick, clothes of the latest design. I'm educated, I work hard and I'm full of confidence. But I live for tenderness. 'Such talk,' I'd say, curling into the heat of his body.

He still worried, at that time, about fulfilling his duties as a caretaker. 'I should get an office posting,' he'd say to me after we made love. 'I should support both of us, not rely on your store to feed us.'

'You'll get a job soon,' I always assured him. 'With your high-school degree, your charm. You'll work one day at an office, just you wait and see.'

'What it takes is connections,' my husband would say. 'And those, we don't have.'

Dhan Raj Kafle, the peon at the Computer Centre, was a wrinkled old man in eternally crusty clothes, who seemed, at first glance, resigned to the menial tasks of making tea, running personal errands for his bosses, delivering the mail. But like anyone he had needs, desires, and family demands to fulfil. He was looking out for better opportunities, to become a bit more secure, eat just a little better—who wasn't? He hoped one day to be able to afford an English-medium boarding school for his eldest son.

One late spring day, Dhan Raj was delivering the mail, shuffling from one office to another, when he noticed a letter for Kamal Malla Sir from a foreign country. He used his fourth-grade English to make out the word Thailand, and reflected that it was irregular for a letter to go straight to Kamal Sir without going through the higher-up bosses. Dhan Raj was due for a raise. In order to demonstrate his loyalty to the supervisor, he took the letter to him, and said, 'This is from abroad.' How was he to know that the supervisor begrudged others prospects better than his own?

Kamal finally tired of waiting in thrall for his dreams, and telephoned Hrishikesh to invite him for a beer. Not that he could afford it. His salary at the Computer Centre was four thousand rupees a month; one Iceberg was seventy rupees. But he felt defiant. He was college-educated, young—at twenty-six—and capable. If nothing ever came of the Asian Institute of Technology—AIT, AIT—he could resign from work and start a business—maybe a computer store—to support himself anyhow. And if worst came to worst, he'd do what it took: he'd become a partner in his uncle's new bakery.

'The same place?' Hrishikesh asked over the phone, and Kamal said, 'Somewhere else. Somewhere I've never been. You decide.'

Hrishikesh suggested the San Francisco Yeti Pizza Hut. Kamal didn't know where it was, and at half past six he stopped by my store to ask for directions. He addressed me politely as an older sister, and spoke in a low, modulated voice. I told him to walk due east till he reached the Rum Doodle Bar, then take a left towards the Pilgrim's Book Store, if he knew where that was. He said yes. He was early, so he bought a pack of cigarettes, lit up slowly and lingered outside my store, his shapely features lit up by the blue of a neon sign on the store next door. It was a warm evening, and the crowds of tourists were thick, babbling, colourful, brimming with an otherworldly energy. I watched Kamal walk slowly, with his characteristic poise, into the clutter of foreign souls.

At the San Francisco Yeti Pizza Hut, Kamal found Hrishikesh waiting at a table by the window, looking on to tangled electrical lines. He ordered a beer, and Hrishikesh ordered Sprite, and they decided to share a Hawaiian pizza. Kamal had never eaten a Hawaiian pizza before. He asked about Hrishikesh's work, but found the responses vague, evasive. So he talked about his sister's wedding. But Hrishikesh seemed distracted. During a lull in the conversation, Hrishikesh tilted his head and hummed along with the song playing over the restaurant's tape recorder, 'Taking a ride—on a cosmic train.'

'Cat Stevens,' Kamal said, remembering the name. 'I used to listen to it in India.'

Hrishikesh was surprised to discover that Kamal had done his bachelor's in computer science in Madras, South India. Somehow he had thought Kamal had never left Nepal. He listened to the other man speak in a suddenly unfamiliar way. 'Some of the college boys listen to wild, wild songs,' Kamal said, thinking back to his youth. 'Pink Floyd, Led Zeppelin, Uriah Heep. I never went wild, but some of them these boys were wild.'

'Uriah Heep?'

Kamal sat forward, lit a cigarette and followed the lead of the memories that unfolded. 'They went,' he said, ignoring the pineapple-strewn pizza that the waiter put down, 'those Indian boys, they went to the States and Britain and Australia to work after college. I also wanted to go, but my parents. They are getting old and I am the only son. They need me. Some of the boys went to do PhD, even. I have one classmate went to a place called University of Pennsylvania.'

'U Penn,' Hrishikesh said. 'That's close to Boston, the place my parents live. Maybe six hours' drive.'

'He is a brilliant boy,' Kamal said, getting agitated. He stubbed out his cigarette and said emphatically, 'My parents are proud I am a computer engineer. It is a big thing for them. But if I have to spend my life at this kind of job, doing nothing, earning one-two thousand, I feel why I studied? Why I worked so hard?' He tried to smile, but couldn't, and continued, 'I don't want to spend my life thinking twice before having a cup of coffee. Even ten rupees is a big thing when you work in the government.'

Then, composing himself, he laughed, but Hrishikesh, watching closely, could see that his mirth wasn't earnest. Kamal frowned again and said, 'What kind of life is that?' Then he lowered his voice and revealed to Hrishikesh his secret: that he had applied to AIT in Bangkok. 'Very good university,' he said. 'Most of the graduates they go to work in Australia later. Australian companies come to recruit us, even.'

The Cat Stevens tape ended, and was replaced by the screech of Nirvana.

'Australia.' Hrishikesh was disappointed that Kamal was less Nepali than he'd appeared to be. He said, 'Though Kathmandu's not that bad, if you think about it. Sometimes I think it's just our attitude, you know? If we could simplify our life, get back to basics…' Then he began to talk about his yoga classes, and the amazing, expanding effect meditation had had on his consciousness. 'It's like we need to find all the good parts of being Nepali,' he said, cringing at the clumsy sound of his words. 'Without all that shit about the caste system and all, you know.' He frowned, and his bony, angled features suddenly looked very strict to Kamal. Hrishikesh went on, 'It was the Brahmin pundits who reinterpreted Hinduism so that it would benefit them. They began the caste system and all. But things like yoga, like meditation—they're timeless.'

Kamal couldn't quite follow what Hrishikesh was saying. 'But you are also speaking like a real Brahmin,' he said, laughing.

'I was always sort of interested in my roots,' Hrishikesh said solemnly. 'In college I read the Upanishads and Vedas, and practised Ayurveda. Now that I'm meditating, I'm beginning to find something I like—that's ours, truly ours.' He noticed the quizzical expression on Kamal's face and suddenly let go of his thoughts. 'Yeah, I guess I am speaking like a Brahmin.'

'You have to put all traditions and crap behind you,' Kamal said in a tone that he hoped sounded neutral. As a gesture of friendship he offered Hrishikesh a cigarette.

'None for me,' Hrishikesh said. 'I'm cutting down; it isn't good for you.'

'You talk like a hippy American,' Kamal said.

Hrishikesh noticed that there was an edge of argument to the rest of their conversation. Every time he mentioned yoga or meditation, Kamal seemed to smile sardonically. Hrishikesh countered by lecturing briefly, when they parted, that Nepal wasn't a bad place to live. 'It's all in our minds,' he said. 'This city is what we make of it.'

How would he know, Kamal mused as they took leave; Hrishikesh had only lived here a few months, and could leave any time he wanted.

They met again the next week for lunch at the Laughing Buddha Thai Restaurant. Hrishikesh invited Kamal this time, after realizing that he shouldn't have judged his friend's desire to go to Bangkok. Why shouldn't he go, Hrishikesh had realized. We all need to see the world, and return to Nepal out of our own free will. If we want to return.

Kamal had also regretted his comments about Hrishikesh's spirituality. Their friendship was too nice to treat so thoughtlessly. After all, he had no one else with whom he could talk like this. In all his other relationships, Kamal acted out the roles defined for him by society. Hrishikesh was free, like an American, and he lent Kamal some of his freedom. The least Kamal could do was support Hrishikesh in his desire to be a different kind of Hindu, or whatever he wanted to be.

These warm impulses Thamel encouraged. The Laughing Buddha Thai Restaurant was bright and lively, with its chequered linoleum floors and clashing tablecloths and pulsating Hindi love songs. At the start both friends listened respectfully to each other, trying to make the other feel comfortable. When it came their turn to talk, they willed themselves to be open and trustful. Quickly enough they settled into an easy, rambling conversation about anything that came to mind: family obligations, politics, childhood events, the software industry, journalism, the electricity shortage. As the afternoon progressed, Kamal raised his beer and Hrishikesh his Pepsi, and they toasted their unknown futures.

Afterwards they stopped by Kuber Sharma's shop and bought a sweetmeat each; their mouths were thick with syrup when they said farewell.

It was then that their lives diverged. Kamal decided that, as it was May, he should fax AIT's admissions officer, a Mrs B. Sirichanda whose signature was decorated with ornate curlicues. He received a reply—unsigned, from the Admissions Office—that they had given his seat to someone else because he had not responded on time. They wished him the best in his education.

Stunned, he called up AIT. 'I did not received your any admission letter,' he cried into the telephone, but the response from the other side was unwavering.

For days Kamal walked about in a daze, doing no work, questioning everyone at work about a letter from Thailand—had they seen it anywhere? The peon Dhan Raj Kafle, who had got his raise and who harboured no particular resentment against Kamal Sir, told him that he thought he'd seen such a letter on the supervisor's desk.

Kamal staggered. There were those Nepalis, he knew, who harmed others because they had to, competing for the same limited resources. Then there were those, like the supervisor, who harmed others purely because they wanted to; envy rotted their heart, led them to hold down everyone who might rise above them.

Kamal saw his future slip away. In the harsh hours of a

sleepless dawn, he cursed his luck, his society, and his parents, whose traditional expectations of him had jinxed him. And he railed against his sister, whose narrow, duty-bound world he was now trapped in. He was so wracked by fury, he didn't want to continue at work.

Hrishikesh, meanwhile, had realized that he hated Nepal. This insight came the day the *Kathmandu Newsflash* received the first Letter to the Editor objecting to his weekly articles about true versus false Hinduism. The letter was cranky, but what upset Hrishikesh the most was the fact that the editor, R. P. Aryal, had insisted on printing it the very next day. Surely he could have delayed it a little, or not printed it at all. Most of the paper's letters were faked by the staff anyway.

Another letter had come in the next day's mail, also criticizing Hrishikesh's articles. The next one that had come was personal in tone. 'We don't need a Green Card Holding Boy to telling us our religion,' a certain Manamohan Dhungel had written on a laser-printed note. 'Please you tell him that if he lives in Nepal all his life, only then he wills unedrstand what it is Hinduism. Not this superfacial dharma-talk from America.'

R. P. Aryal had printed that letter too, with undue haste.

Hrishikesh had tried not to give any of this significance, but he just couldn't ignore the way his colleagues turned around to watch him as he passed. It almost seemed like these people despised him. What harm had he done? Or perhaps he was being too sensitive... He had tried to remind himself to always breathe from his stomach, but had grown tired, soon enough, of constantly shielding himself from the—perhaps imagined— hostility of those around him.

He had called up his parents in Boston and mentioned that he might come back.

Kamal noticed that Hrishikesh's name had disappeared from the *Kathmandu Newsflash* masthead, but he was too busy helping set up his uncle's bakery—and too unhappy—to call. A week later, Hrishikesh called the Computer Centre, and found out that Kamal had resigned. Hrishikesh didn't have Kamal's home number. So, in a Nepali enough gesture, he dropped by his house, and left word with Kamal's elderly parents that he was leaving the country.

The next week, Kamal and Hrishikesh met at the Third World European Cuisine—where the waiter Lal Bahadur Rai mistook Hrishikesh, who arrived first, for a foreigner, because what kind of Nepali wears wrinkled orange pyjamas? 'You like to make pretty wife, sir?' Lal Bahadur asked, and was extremely embarrassed when Hrishikesh responded, 'Ma Nepali hun.' The waiter reddened, then asked abruptly what Hrishikesh wanted to drink. Luckily, another man soon joined him—now *he* was clearly Nepali—and Lal Bahadur took their orders and retreated to the kitchen.

For this, their last meeting, both friends were careful to be respectful, and attentive to each other's plight. Each listened carefully to the other, praised his recent decisions, assuring him that the path he had chosen would lead in the right direction.

'You go to America,' Kamal said in an assuring tone. 'You take a job nicely, and be free, and become a Hindu saint if you want. It is much better than wasting a rotten life here. You don't know,' he smiled to soften his point, 'how small-small people think here, how they destroy others to make themself feel good.'

'And you,' Hrishikesh said, his voice full of conviction. 'You should reapply to AIT next year. They'll accept you, with your experience, your background, your promise. Think this way: you're only delaying your plans by a year.'

Kamal, who had spent all day among the muffins, cakes, apple pies, turnovers and strudels at his uncle's bakery, appreciated this thought.

It was rare, both men realized, to find a friend like this. They held hands warmly when they took leave. And in the following years they sent each other a postcard, a letter, some newspaper clippings, then stopped corresponding eventually, but always took strength from the thought that the other was out there, somewhere, a source of goodwill in the world.

Or maybe they remained fast friends. Maybe Hrishikesh sent Kamal computer magazines with ads for technical schools, and Kamal applied and got a scholarship and left Nepal. Or maybe Kamal sent Hrishikesh news of a United Nations position that had opened up here, and Hrishikesh applied and got the job and came back to Nepal.

It doesn't actually matter, because I made them both up. A woman sitting in a shop all day needs stories. But this is a real story, meaning: true to my desire. I sit here all day long, and want Nepalis, like foreigners, to meet each other in wonder in Thamel—to forge the heart connections we don't in our own society. Why are we, among ourselves, jealous and resentful, mistrustful of everyone? Why can we not become friends the way foreigners can—full of goodness and grace? This is what I want.

What I have is something else—a life filled with debt and obligation. These days it seems to me that my fortunes have become as changeling as my neighbour Tenzing Namgyal's views on god. My husband has given up hope of ever finding an office job. He drinks too much at night, speaks harshly and doesn't help out at the shop in the daytime. Alone all day, I now sell books, magazines and tapes—and also Johnson and Johnson sunblock cream, Nescafé, Kraft cheese, Pantene Pro-V shampoo. But I still can't pay back our debts.

Every week I visit Dilip Basnyat, trying to postpone our loan payments. Afterwards I stop by the kitchen to see his cook, my cousin. My poor, ailing cousin. He is all dry bones now. He is my father's own sister's son—but sometimes I wish he'd die soon. It will avenge me, his death. It will ruin La Vie Boheme, and Dilip Basnyat will see that even he is not safe from misfortune. I do not like having such hard thoughts. How I want my cousin to die.

Three Hundred Rupees

~

Rohit's eyes were open but he wasn't seeing much: a haze of trees, a blur of blocky buildings, the yellow-blue hues of dawn, Kathmandu. He was tired of the way the bus rattled his bones and sick of the two prattling women behind him, who had talked non-stop throughout the night. 'Look,' one of them said now, as they passed a vast, tarred lot filled with colourful cars, 'it's like a garden made of metal.'

'All those lamps on the roads,' said the other woman. 'And they won't give our village even one bulb! And look at those houses, they're all offices.'

'So many offices. What do people do in them?'

'They sit at tables and claim to be developing our country. Look how wide the road is.'

'So many motor cars. Where do they go at night?'

'To the stalls of their owners.'

The bus swerved sharply and shuddered to a halt. Rohit stood up, anxious to leave. Was this the bus park? Outside the windows was a row of buses: yes. He looped his black-and-white book bag across his shoulders and jostled past the other passengers as they were standing up. A woman clucked, 'Tch,' as he brushed against her. 'What's the rush,' someone groused. He paid them no mind and sidled up to the conductor, a boy of about twelve with a smile too sly on his lips. 'Open the door,' he urged the boy. 'Why don't you open the door?'

The boy kicked open the door and out stepped Rohit dressed in a wrinkled blue tunic, traditional close-fitting trousers, a flower-patterned cap and Chinese cloth shoes that sold for seventy-five rupees in the village. To stave off Kathmandu's blistering fog he had worn a black waistcoat and a scratchy muffler. His face was dark, and his hands were rough from farm work.

He noticed that his breath was a white evaporating cloud, and everything smelled of greased machines in the nation's capital. He walked to a large building with square glass windows and stopped in front of the door. A row of buses was parked there. Some of them were local, he knew, and others went all over the country. A shiver of pleasure at the vastness of the world swept through him. There were so many places he hadn't been to: the horizonful of farmlands in the south, the clipped, tidy tea estates in the east. And beyond that, India. Everyone and their sons went to India to work these days.

He approached an emerald-green bus. A young man was standing beside it. 'I needed to get to a place called Chettrapati,' Rohit said to him.

The young man, who was wearing very high-quality modern jean-pants, pointed with his chin across the road. 'Chettrapati bus is over there.'

Rohit looked across the road. There were no buses there, just a row of three-wheel auto-rikshaas. Still, the young man had sounded sure of himself, so Rohit made his way over to the rikshaas, stopping at the first one. He said to the driver, 'I needed to get to a place called Chettrapati.'

The driver was wearing dark glasses. He mumbled something that Rohit didn't understand, then leaned back and pushed open the canvas door. Rohit climbed in head, arms and legs first. 'Close the door,' the driver said, and Rohit obeyed. The inside of the rikshaa was lively, with red-and-yellow linoleum mats. The walls were plastered with pictures, pictures of— naked women. Rohit's first thought was: how shameful! What if he had come with his wife, or daughters? How humiliating that would have been! Shyly, he examined the pictures. One particularly salacious drawing had a naked woman holding a giant cigarette between her legs.

The rikshaa started up with a roar and lurched on to the road. It steered itself out of the bus park and towards the city, which was hidden behind the fog. Rohit vaguely remembered this stretch from the first trip he had taken to Kathmandu last year with his brother. It had been like this then too: trucks and buses had showed up suddenly and disappeared into the fog.

'Coming for a visit?' the driver shouted above the racket of his rikshaa engine.

Rohit hmm'ed, slightly hesitant to talk to a man who kept pictures of naked women in his rikshaa. But he was of gregarious temperament, so he couldn't help adding, 'I've got relatives here.'

'Your son?' The driver leaned out and spat, and Rohit saw the saliva streak past him.

He too leaned out and spat. The wind whipped his face. He drew back and said, 'My brother. He moved here a year ago.'

'I've got a son,' the driver said. 'Studying at the campus. Day after day I drive past his dormitory, but don't stop to see him. Know why?' He turned back briefly, giving a profile view of his dark glasses. 'His friends will laugh because I'm a rikshaa driver. Imagine that! Can you imagine that?'

Rohit clucked. 'Unthinkable.'

'Is that how a son should think?' The rikshaa swerved into a narrow alley. 'Is that how your own son should think?'

Rohit's infant son in the village was all laughter, cries, gurgles, shit and piss. 'That's not how a son should think,' he said.

'How many sons do you have?'

'One,' Rohit said. 'And four girls.'

'Where?'

'Just outside Dhorphirdi.'

The driver shrugged.

'In Tanahun district,' Rohit said. 'An hour off the road. Driest patch of land you ever saw—can't farm a crop! The bus stops right at the bridge to Dhorphirdi.'

The rikshaa puttered to a sudden halt. 'Here's Chettrapati,' said the driver.

Peering out, Rohit saw that they were hemmed in on all sides by narrow cement buildings. 'Oho,' he exclaimed. 'Look at all these houses. How will I find my brother? Who are all these people? Do they live in these houses? Look at that girl with white hair! What happened to her?'

'She's a foreigner. Forty-two rupees.'

'Forty-two!'

'What I said when you got in.'

Preposterous! 'One rupee fifty,' Rohit cried. 'That's how

much it's meant to be. I came here last year and took a similar rikshaa, don't think I don't know anything.'

'This is a private rikshaa,' the driver said, turning back to glare at Rohit through his dark glasses. The glasses gave him a menacing, insect-like expression. 'Look at the meter: it says forty-two rupees.'

'That's enough to feed a whole family!'

'Forty, then.'

'Taking advantage of innocent villagers,' Rohit complained, but he realized there was nothing to do but pay. He took a long time finding a fifty-rupee bill and waited morosely as the driver counted change. A thief of a place, this city. And so noisy, so full of people whose heads bobbed up and down, up and down the streets. He looked again at the white-haired woman and wondered why, if she was foreign, there was a ring in her nose. The driver nudged him to attention, handed back a bill and leaned back to open the door for him.

Rohit hadn't quite stepped out when the rikshaa revved up again and chased off after a car. He took a firm hold of his black-and-white book bag and looked around. He must find a rest spot with a green tin awning. Green tin awning, he'd been told. Young men, old men, women of all ethnicities passed by in a swirl of colours. Look, Rohit said to himself, middle-aged women wearing pants.

Then he saw, across the road, a high covered platform at the centre of traffic, and it had a green tin awning. Chettrapati. He stepped towards it and felt a warm, soft body and the sudden metal edges of a bicycle. 'Don't you have eyes!' someone yelled. A horn honked. A few cars swept by. A large man shoved him off the sidewalk. Rohit waited till the road was completely clear and ran through safely to the covered platform.

A few men were lying down on the platform's bare cement floor. Tch: how cold they must be, he thought. By their features he thought they might be Tamangs. Porters. They were holding on to ropes to carry their loads with. Rohit squatted down beside them, trying to imagine the life of a city porter. It would be like trekking-company porters, only they would be carrying chairs, desks, cupboards from truck to truck, shop to shop, one merchant to another. What would make a man want to live that kind of life? A flood in his village maybe, or landslides that wiped away his house and fields. Some of Rohit's fields had been destroyed over the last monsoon. But the gods had blessed him and his brother with a whole hillside of terraced farmlands, part of which he had just sold at his brother's insistence.

The fog seemed to thicken and a silver mist rolled through the street, swirling along with the commotion of the street. The cold of the platform stiffened Rohit's bones. He drew his muffler over his nose to savour the warmth of his own breath. A long time, maybe an hour, passed as he distracted himself with the sights that passed before him. Why, he wondered, did motorcycles make such a racket, while cars glided by so silently? How much would all the signboards on this street cost to make, combined? If everyone all over Nepal stopped farming and came to the city, what would people eat?

'Uncle,' he heard eventually, and turned to see a thin boy dressed in a blue school uniform, standing a little way off.

It was Keshab. 'Nephew,' he said, standing up. 'Come and pay your respects to your old uncle. How tall you've grown, how like a city boy.' He held out his hand in blessing, but noticed a reluctance in the boy's motions as he bowed. 'Where's your father?' Rohit asked. 'How far is his shop?'

The boy pointed vaguely towards one of the intersecting roads, then began to head towards it.

Rohit followed him. 'What do you have in that nice school bag?' he said, trying to win the boy's affection. 'Books that teach you English?'

But Keshab said nothing, slipping so fast through the crowd that Rohit had to hurry to keep pace.

'You must be the tallest boy in your class,' Rohit called out after his nephew, but Keshab just ducked into a dark, unpaved alley.

At the end of the alley they reached a temple. There the alley opened up to a large heavily trafficked pitched road. An ambulance raced by on it, wailing like a widow in grief. Rohit stuck close to his nephew as they darted through the traffic across. On the other side was a pavement full of street vendors selling shirts, caps, peanuts, vegetables and fruit.

Keshab stopped and pointed further up along the sidewalk. 'There's Baba, over there.'

And there he was, Narayan, sitting at the centre of a concentric display of bananas. Narayan saw him and lifted a hand. Rohit noticed that his brother didn't rise in greeting, let alone bow, when he walked up to him. He tried not to mind this oversight. His brother had lost the tanned complexion of a villager and his face was as pale as wheat. His hair was combed back and oiled and he wore a fancy acrylic sweater and impressively clean trousers of terry-cotton. The transformations people go through in a year! If it weren't for the dent in both their noses, Rohit thought, no one could tell that they were the same father's sons.

His nephew had disappeared, and for a while Rohit just stood on the pavement, hovering over his brother's concentric display of bananas.

'Sit,' Narayan finally suggested, and so Rohit squatted beside the bananas, holding on to his book bag.

'Sit more comfortably,' Narayan insisted with a hint of annoyance in his voice, so Rohit gathered together his blue tunic and settled into the gritty pavement. His brother, he saw, was sitting on a straw mat. The protocol was all wrong. Pretending not to notice this affront, Rohit turned with a keen, interested expression to study his surroundings. A dim sun was finally glowing through the fog, putting a glint in the glass, steel and mica city. The building across the street had windows like dark mirrors. On the road there were so many cars packed together, inching along like a metal snake. 'Where does that go?' Rohit asked pointing at a manhole cover, then answered his own question, 'To the sewers beneath, of course.' When fashionable ladies walked by, he noticed, their high-heel shoes clacked against the pavement. He finally turned to his brother. 'How much do your bananas sell for?'

'I take what I can get.' Narayan's tone was flat. 'Do you want some? Are you hungry?'

'So early in the morning,' Rohit demurred, too proud to admit to hunger in the face of such lack of ceremony. He smiled wanly. 'Nobody eats at such an early hour.'

'Did you bring the money?'

This was why Rohit had never liked Narayan. His brother

didn't have the least courtesy; he didn't show any consideration for anyone. He was crass; he was greedy. It had been like this since childhood: his brother had been the spoiled, overindulged younger child. Rohit reached into his book bag and took out a roll of bank notes. 'Fifteen thousand,' he said, giving it to Narayan. 'That's your share.'

With a sly innuendo, his brother said, 'I heard land was selling for twice this much at Khaireni.'

'Are we Khaireni?' Rohit snapped. 'Has the government dug a road all the way to our house? Have they brought us electricity?' He watched Narayan tuck the money into his acrylic sweater. 'You forget our fields are mostly sand. And with the landslides last monsoon...'

Narayan sank back on his straw mat, his face spoiling. 'Everyone thinks,' he spat out, 'that I have it good in the city. I'm earning, my wife's earning, my son's in school, I don't have troubles of my own.' He gestured contemptuously at the concentric display of bananas, and seemed to want to say something more, but didn't.

Rohit could hardly believe what he was hearing. 'Are you suggesting I'm cheating you?' He reached into his black-and-white book bag and pulled out the land sales deed. 'Signed by the secretary of the Village Development Committee!' He waved the paper in front of his brother. 'Look for yourself and see how much money I've robbed you of—thousands and thousands of rupees!'

Instead of bowing in shame, Narayan grabbed the paper and began to look over it.

The gall of the boy! Had he forgotten all the times Rohit had washed him, fed him, clothed him, mended his pants, defended him from bigger boys, sheltered him from their stepmother's wrath? All the times he'd taken the cows to graze so that his brother could attend school? It was Rohit's sacrifices that had made Narayan turn out so smart and city-slick now. Rohit wanted to remind his brother of all these sacrifices, but just then a woman came up to the display of bananas, all fluttering nylon sari and flowers in her hair.

Narayan put aside the sales deed and sold her a dozen bananas. Both brothers watched as the woman walked mincingly away in her high-heel shoes. The flowers in her hair, Rohit saw, were of plastic.

Narayan finally handed the land sales deed back to Rohit. For a while both brothers sat huffed in hostility, their expressions equally hard. Rohit eventually started to shiver from the cold. He shifted and coughed to cover the sound of his stomach growling.

Finally Narayan mumbled something about tea and got up, and went to a nearby tea stall. Rohit watched his brother waiting in line to buy tea, and he suddenly felt filled with remorse. For some reason it was sad, this sight. Where was his sister-in-law? Where had his nephew disappeared? Why not invite him to their dwellings and serve a proper meal there? Rohit was himself keen to see their lodgings—built of cement, it would surely be better than the old clay hut in the village.

Narayan came back with two glasses of black tea, which they both sipped in silence. The hot drink soothed the cold and eased Rohit's hunger. It also seemed to soften the expression on Narayan's face.

Presently, Rohit asked, 'And Keshab's mother, where is she?'

'She works at a factory.' Narayan's tone was conciliatory. 'Otherwise she'd cook a meal for you in our rented room.'

'What kind of rent do you pay?'

'A thousand a month.'

'A thousand!' Rohit felt a pang of guilt about the eight thousand rupees he'd kept for himself by forging the land sales deed. Eight months of rent in this city. He gulped down the rest of his tea, suddenly wanting to get out of Kathmandu, and return to his own Dhorphirdi.

'I should get back to the bus park,' he said. His knees cracked volubly as he stood. 'There's a meeting tonight—about the broken irrigation canal...I mustn't be late for it.'

Of course Narayan didn't insist he stay on. He actually looked relieved. 'I'll show you the right bus,' he said.

He took Rohit by the arm and led him further up the pavement to a four-way intersection. There he showed him to a battered blue mini-bus. 'Sit next to the window so you can see where you are. Get off at the bus park and ask at the ticket booth for the Pokhara bus.'

Rohit hoisted himself on to the mini-bus. The front of the bus was empty, but the aisle was crowded with nubile girls in starched college uniforms. It would be awkward to push through them to get to those seats. So Rohit remained by the door, clutching a window bar for support.

'Dai,' Narayan called out from the door, reaching in to slip some soft money-textured notes into Rohit's hand. 'You must be...I couldn't even feed you. And the bus fare...such a long trip.' He said, 'There are restaurants by the bus park.'

Embarrassed, Rohit shoved the money into his book bag.

Then a man clambered into the bus, knocking against Rohit. 'Room, I need some room,' he said. 'Can you move a little?' Once on board, he reached down and pulled up two bleating goats. Rohit pressed against the side of the bus to make room for them, then followed the man and his goats past the nubile college girls.

At the front of the bus he took a window-side seat. He turned back to wave at Narayan, but it seemed that his brother had already left.

The man with the goats sat across the aisle from Rohit.

Rohit looked over the goats. 'Such goats,' he said appreciatively as the animals bleated. 'Are you going to sell them in the bazaar?'

'If I get my price,' the man responded. 'Only if I get my price.'

'And how much will this one go for?' He pointed at the bigger goat.

The man reached into his coat pocket and took out a cigarette. 'I'll take what I get,' he said, after he lit up. 'Eight-nine hundred, a thousand. Twelve hundred. Depending.'

'Twelve hundred!' Rohit leaned over and plucked a hair from the goat's rump. The animal bristled. He inspected the root of the follicle. 'There isn't even that much fat on it,' he said.

'I'll take what I can get,' the man repeated. The smell of his cigarettes made Rohit realize how hungry he was. The man's muffler was of the same scratchy material as his own, but cleaner. The man's pants were of thick black wool. He was wearing shoes, but no socks. Or no: he was wearing socks the same colour as skin.

Tilled Earth

The bus started up with a rumble. Rohit sat back in his seat, examining the skin-coloured socks: if he hadn't looked closely he wouldn't have seen its fine ribs.

As the bus lurched on to the road, Rohit was suffused with a sense of mystery at all the things there were in cities like this that looked one way, but acted differently. All the fronts and illusions. Look at Narayan: the boy was so rude, so coarse, but he knew in his heart that he owed Rohit everything. He knew he owed his elder brother his whole life. In his heart, Narayan knew. He didn't show it, but he knew. How could he not know?

Rohit checked in his book bag to see how much money his brother had given him.

Three hundred rupees.

Three hundred rupees.

He counted again. Three hundred rupees.

Was that too much or too little? As the bus lurched on its way, Rohit turned to the owner of the goats. 'How many meals do three hundred rupees buy in this city, our nation's capital?'

Diesel

~

*On his way back from the hospital, Jitendra saw a flock of red-*whiskered bulbuls in the oak tree in his front garden. When his wife asked what the doctors had said, he just laughed: 'There's too much carbon monoxide in the city air.' That evening, looking out of the window, Jitendra saw the red-whiskered bulbuls again. He realized that they were nesting in the oak tree.

It was the dust, he thought, kicked up by vehicle wheels: that was the biggest problem in this city. The soot and dust. The next day, at the office, he mentioned to a colleague that if he were an environmentalist he would have all the city's dirt roads pitched, and all its empty lots covered with grass. Though that wouldn't remove the toxic particulates—polyaromatic hydrocarbon, nitrogen dioxide, sulphur oxide—already in his lungs. He thought of all the cars, buses, jeeps, two-stroke motorbikes and three-wheelers in the city. He had so loved the sweet musk of diesel as a child.

On his way to the hospital that evening he saw a blue-throated barbet on a dead pine tree. He was waiting for the bus on the traffic-clogged main street when this happened. The iridescent bird gleamed against the dull bark. How birds live, he thought, in this smog.

That night he told his wife the doctors had confirmed that there was a shadow in his right lung.

'Did they say it was dangerous?'

'They took a second set of X-rays.'

Early the next morning Jitendra stole away to the nearby Gaushala forest, binoculars in hand. It was birds he wanted to see, and birds he saw in the dawn light: honey kites, rose-ringed parakeets, robin dayals, a hoopoe and several ashy drongoes. How do these birds fare, he wondered, amid all the toxic particulates? In a thicket he sighted a tiny olive-hued bird that looked like a fluttering birch leaf. Green warbler. It darted from branch to branch, then flitted away. It did not look diseased. None of these birds looked diseased. He did not feel diseased. All the cars, buses, jeeps, two-stroke motorbikes and three-wheelers in this city. How he had loved the sweet musk of diesel as a child.

I Don't Like Shanta Khanal

~

I don't like Shanta Khanal because she steals books from other girls when no one's looking. At recess we play marbles in the schoolyard and our sir doesn't let us talk in the classroom. Yesterday I won a red marble, but I like my green ones better so I'll trade it for Nanu's. Sir hits us on the head with a ruler if we don't know the correct maths answers. We have to carry our books with us during recess, or Shanta Khanal will steal them, especially if the books are new; but if you tear the cover off they'll look old, and no one will steal them. Kopila's book got stolen once and her mother had to buy her another one; that's sixty rupees, fifty if you go to the government store. Her mother beat her so hard. They sell bubble gum at the temple-side shop. Sometimes we stop there after school and buy things; if you've got eleven rupees you can buy coconut biscuits, that's my favourite. The shopkeeper's mother is a witch. Yesterday everyone else stole oranges from her backyard, but I was too scared so I stayed outside the yard. Sir never punishes Shanta Khanal because she knows all the maths answers. I can say my five times tables faster than her, though. Nanu kept saying, 'Come into the yard, there's a whole tree full of oranges, and they're ripe and ready to eat,' but I was too scared, and it's wrong to steal. I'm this much taller than Nanu, Kopila's shorter than her and Dalli's even shorter. This morning sir hit Dalli on the head for not knowing the prime minister's name; I don't know it either. The other day a gang of boys attacked the sir from class five; he's in the hospital now, in bandages. Five twos are ten, five fives are twenty. Sir said Karl Marx killed a thousand people and all the teachers are going on strike next month if they don't get bigger salaries. The other day one sir made a boy sit like a chicken: that's when you sit and put your arms through your knees, and hold your ears, so you look like a chicken. We all laughed at the boy, who was so stupid he cried. Sir goes to Shanta Khanal's house twice a week to coach her at maths, her house is on the hill and her father's even got a taxi. After school one day last week, Nanu, Kopila, Dalli and I went to the haunted house in the fairground; entrance is two rupees. The ghost had red eyes and blue hair, but I wasn't scared of him, and kept lifting his robe and shouting, 'You're not a real ghost, you're a person.' Nanu said, 'What kind of ghost wears sandals?' When you're stealing oranges, if the witch catches you she'll suck your blood till you die. Kopila says she's seen the witch kill babies. I have to do my homework tonight because sir said he'll ask me what four plus six is, and won't let me count on my fingers. There's a dancing monkey by the temple which cries if you hit it, but you have to pay one rupee first. Shanta Khanal gets better grades than us because her father pays for private tuition. I stole her maths book at recess when no one was looking. It was so new. She wears nice blue ribbons in her hair and I want them. How can anyone kill a thousand people without anyone noticing? Five ones are five, five twos are ten. My mother said she'd take me to see the dancing monkey later today, do you want to come along?

Tilled Earth

Love Marriage

~

Say there are a lot of vases in the shopfront catching the sunlight,
casting shadows that confuse you and you can't tell if you want
the one with the slight curve and flower design or the square
one because they look the same and if you don't look closely
you can't tell the difference, let's say. Yesterday a man came in,
took an hour choosing something: but how did he finally know
what he wanted? Sometimes a man comes in, looks at every
shirt, fountain pen, watch, photo frame before choosing a pair
of socks, maybe…but how do you know, do you think, if
you've selected the right item if you walk in and point at the
first thing that catches your eye? Do you just know?

Lalita, you'd scoff if you heard me say that. You'd call me
stupid, you'd argue, fighting my words as I speak, or before,
even—it's like you wait to correct anything I say, so I don't say
anything because I know you're right, but if you'd listen to
me…I know girls aren't like vases for sale in a shopfront. That's
what you'd argue and you'd be right, but it's not what I mean,
you won't hear me out.

The first girl I saw was Monica Karki, the colonel's daughter,
and she was all right, but I didn't marry her, did I? It was last

summer, and there was a servant boy who showed us into her father's house, and there were marble floors, framed certificates behind glass, seashells on the shelf from Lebanon maybe, where they say the colonel made his fortune. Uncle and I looked at the vase of fat red dahlias and waited. The colonel—was he busy that day, was he posturing, did he mean to show us how important he was when he stepped into the room so late? Why was he in full uniform? 'Sit, please, please. No need to stand. Do forgive me for being so late.' To me he said, 'And you're the young man, Bimal.'

Was there anything to say, should I have said something? I just nodded.

He turned to uncle. 'Your own nephew, Damodar?'

Uncle tried his best to be chatty, which he isn't naturally, 'My own brother's son,' he said. 'His one and only. Helps out at his father's factory. Runs it, practically. Excellent manager.'

The colonel turned back and looked at the coat I was wearing. He said, 'So sorry to hear of your mother's demise. Such a charming lady. She was, as you know, my own sister's very good friend.'

Was there anything to do but nod?

Later, I blamed the coat. Sometimes you make one bad choice, like a coat that's too big, and wool, I mean it had to be my winter coat; why didn't I wear my father's lighter ones? The heat prickled against the inside of my arms, and the whole time that's all I could think about. A girl's lipstick, it doesn't help either when it's not the right colour. Uncle was saying things about my father's business—'My brother just came back from Dhaka, will leave for Osaka, so successful, our Bimal helps out, stiff, the competition.' The colonel murmured, and just then his wife and daughter clattered in, high heels, sequins, gauze, gold necklace, jet-black hair, perfume and lipstick the colour of bubble gum.

Nothing I did, nothing worked. You stand, you greet people, you try and look them in the eye, but they overwhelm you with their greetings: 'You really must drop by more often.' 'Such old friends.' 'Where life leads us.' 'Excuse our attire, we're going to a wedding afterwards. Rohit Bajracharya's youngest daughter and a doctor with a green card—there, now, let's have tea.'

Even Monica knew what to do. Serve. She was small—maybe not even five feet—her hair was pinned back, her clothes a blur of purple and when she put my tea cup on the table with a clatter her hands were plump and creamed, like a pastry. That's all I remember. Talk to the girl? The only time I did was when I went to see Karuna Basnet, the girl who was offered to me after Monica. I asked Karuna, 'What's your favourite subject in college?' She whispered, 'Literature.' 'Mine too,' I lied, and asked her who her favourite author was, and she said Shakespeare, but I hadn't read anything by him. Then our parents turned to listen in, and for the rest of the meeting, the girl's face was red. She turned down, and never looked up again. I didn't marry her either.

Lalita, I never knew how to talk. 'I hope there's enough sugar in the tea,' the colonel's wife said brightly, to no one, and then she turned to me and said, 'You take a lot of sugar in your tea, Bimal?'

I said, 'Yes, I do,' and sounded too grave about it.

The colonel's wife blinked. 'Then you may find the tea too

bland. My daughter made it. She doesn't take much sugar. It must be too bland for you—is it, is it too bland for you?'

I said, 'It's just right.'

She said, 'Monica made it.'

Uncle said, 'It's very tasty.'

The mother blinked again. 'She cooks well, too.'

My coat, like a sack, like a shroud; my body, surrounded by the salty grey vapour of my own sweat. The colonel and uncle started talking about where democracy was leading the country and I wanted to look at the girl, but someone might catch me looking, so I didn't, and now I can't remember anything much but how plump, her hands.

There's a beggar girl here who comes to the shop every two or three days, whining for money, one rupee, master, I'm hungry, but she's not here just to beg, she's here to look. Her eyes are wide and they latch on to one thing before gliding on to another, and you can see the hunger in her eyes: it's a hunger for food, but also for the smoothness of glass vases, the plush feel of cotton towels, she hungers to lie down on a spring bed, let's say. Then there'll be a businessman with the same look in his eyes, coming in to buy French underwear, leaving with stop watches, Parker pens—and he'll probably come in next week just to look around again. It's like he never has enough, is never happy with what he's got, wants things but he doesn't know what.

After Monica and Karuna, there was Rekha Chettri, the second daughter of Dhundi Raj Chettri. Rekha managed Bake-Cake, her father's restaurant. Nirmal—you've heard about him, my best friend from before, his mother was Rekha's father's first cousin—Nirmal said Rekha stayed in the store at the beginning of the week. So my other friend Raju and I went to look at her, not that there was serious talk about us. One of her aunts had approached my auntie, but it wasn't clear if she had acted on her own or with the approval of the girl's parents and we didn't know if it meant anything.

Bake-Cake was bright and modern with tiles on the floor and paintings on the wall with pretty village scenes so that everyone can think how beautiful, our country. Rekha wasn't there. We got fruit cakes and tea and sat and stared at three girls at a table—one of them had light, sleepy eyes, and she was sort of attractive.

Rekha finally came in from the kitchen and stood behind the chicken rolls. I told Raju, 'Don't look now, she's come,' but he turned, and we both looked at her. You know how some girls are big-boned so that they look fat but really aren't? Her hair covered one of her eyes like a film star and she wore triangle earrings that looked like plastic. Other than the earrings, she was pretty in a normal sort of way.

Raju turned back with this smile and said, in English, 'Bake-Cake,' in a low tone that implied something dirty. I don't think he would have said that if I'd been serious about the girl, because I wouldn't marry anyone who studied only till high school, no matter how pretty she was—although how can you tell if a girl's pretty after seeing her just that one time, and anyway that doesn't matter. What's she like inside, say? What is she really like? I heard Rekha tell a waiter, 'Refill the vegetable patties.' Then she left the chicken rolls and went back into the kitchen.

A few days later, Raju, Nirmal and I were sitting on the wall across the campus—we were always together those days, we were best friends in fact—and Raju said, 'The girl you marry has to be perfect, so look around, take your time and don't be ruled by your heart.'

'Don't be ruled by your heart?' I said, and he said, he really said, it was stupid, he said, 'Make a checklist and count up each girl's qualities, she has to offer everything, from A to Z.'

And I said, 'No one's perfect.'

Nirmal cut in, 'Raju's got this list.'

Now Nirmal isn't Raju, he isn't handsome and well built and manly, he's a boy, and pale, and too eager to laugh at our jokes. Raju would spend time with us like he was waiting for the next bus; he would leave us when it came. Nirmal, though, lingered. Let's say he faced into the group, and Raju always faced out. And me, and me?

Nirmal got Raju to show me his list, which said, in English, A: attractive. B: beauty, bright. C: charm, cute, class. D: dignity, dainty, doll. E: elegance, all pencilled in on a dirty, crumpled paper.

It was stupid.

Nirmal grinned. 'Perfect wife,' he said, 'Who'd want a wife who doesn't have grace? Doesn't have tenderness?'

I said, 'But what about human qualities? Who'd want a wife without human qualities, but that isn't on the list.'

Raju said, 'So make your own list.'

Nirmal said, 'There's kindness, which means the same thing.'

A group of college girls walked by, and we stopped to look. One of them kept her face turned towards us even after she had passed; she was wearing a bright red blouse. I couldn't help looking at the other ones who'd swept past faster with their heads turned away, and arms stiff by their sides like they were afraid to move. Raju clucked. Nirmal said, 'She's like that heroine Priety' 'Who?' I said, 'Who?' They were talking about the girl in the red blouse, but I didn't know she was a girl Raju liked to look at. I asked what was so perfect about her, 'Does she have A to Z?' Raju just laughed. He was very striking when he laughed like that. A boy like him—tall, well built, rich and handsome—could get married just like that if he wanted. Nirmal said, 'Are you going to marry her?'

Raju said, 'Not if it's an arranged marriage.' Then he said, 'There has to be love.'

That was the first time I thought about how loveless arranged marriages were.

'Love,' Nirmal snickered and nudged me with his elbow.

The girls were getting lost in the crowd, and Raju jumped off the wall and went off after them. Nirmal told me that the girl probably wouldn't marry him anyway. I said, 'Who wouldn't marry Raju?' And I meant it.

Nirmal said, 'She's the daughter of Laxman Khanal, friend. And who is Raju?' He had a point: Raju's father was rich, but he came into money owning a motorcycle workshop, and it was rumoured that he even did some of the work himself maybe, and that wasn't the same as being rich like Laxman Khanal, who opened the first international bank in Kathmandu.

Stupid. People are stupid, we were so stupid, Lalita. We thought F: faithful, friendly, fun, fair. We thought G: grace, good. We thought everything, Lalita, we thought H: healthy, hard-working. I: intimate. J: jentle, just. K: kind. L: laughing, lovely, like. M: merry, makes her husband first. N: nice, noble, nows a lot. O: obedient, orderly. P: pretty, polite, proper. Q: queen. R: rich, right, rose. S: shy, sensitive, sexy. T: tender. U: useful. V: ? W: wonderful. X: ? Y: young. Z: ?

People said that Binita Rawal had a boyfriend in college, and that he left her, and also that she had a long face with eyes set too far apart. Who'd marry a girl like that, except she was the daughter of Dhan Bir Rawal, the former finance secretary—Dhaney, Dhaaney, where's the money?—and after I'd turned down Monica, Karuna and Rekha, my father fixed on Binita Rawal.

I had told uncle that Binita Rawal had had a boyfriend. Father said, 'Those are just rumours,' when uncle raised the point with him. Father even said—really, you know how people think, and this is why I hate him though I shouldn't—he said, 'Dhan Bir's only child, she'll inherit. Also, he can't go on looking at girls forever, what an embarrassment telling the colonel we didn't want his daughter.'

I said, 'She was practically a midget.'

Uncle had read Shakespeare. He said, 'And the Basnet girl—what was wrong with her?'

'Too shy.'

'Shyness is good.'

I pretended I didn't understand. 'Monica wasn't that shy.'

'Is that her name?'

'The colonel's daughter was Monica.'

It was always easy to confuse uncle. He looked at me despondently, with those wet, round eyes of his, the same eyes I catch him looking at me with from across the shop these days, black, and a little sad even when the round rest of him is laughing. I like him so much. And yet, I think, sometimes, I'm afraid…what makes a man make a living off, or build his life upon, let's say, a gift shop, and am I like him? Father being the one who always decided, he said to uncle, 'Your wife says the Rawal girl will be at Kalyan Bikram's son's wedding. Bimal can meet her there, but he'd better buy a suit.'

The way he talked made me think of my mother, crumpled, crushed by the weight of him—she looked like a man, no, a boy, when I slept by her at the Teaching Hospital, ammonia and antiseptic; she looked a little boy when she died.

My father began to say the things he always did and I said the things I did: I can't believe people want me to marry a girl who's had a boyfriend, Love doesn't come before marriage, Binita Rawal's got a long face, And you, you think you're a hero? Which of us looks like a cinema hero? Girls. Girls. You get good returns if you invest properly, and it's time you began to come to the factory, too.

And who am I, Lalita, who will I be, will my face be round like uncle's or lean like my father's? Like his, will my voice hush everyone else? There's a silence in which you can't hear anything, not even outside the window the city's sputtering cars, horn blasts, trucks rumbling and bicycles tinkling, people crying out to greet, to sell. All you hear is what you'd rather have said, what you'd rather say, the silence that hushes the words you're supposed to be hearing, then blares, when all you see is that his mouth is moving familiar. I don't know. Words pass over you without contact. And in the silence you say: I don't want to work at your television factory, that's why I studied civil engineering. What have you done but spent a life assembling TVs? Have you done anything to help the country, second poorest in the world? To help others? To help the nation? I thought to myself then, though I don't now, I'm going to be an engineer, make roads and bridges, do something.

Father was saying, 'Give and take, but always check: what's your profit margin?'

The day after that I saw you, Lalita, and my heart started to pound.

The curves of your back pushing delicately against your dress as you got up and went from one vendor to another, checking sweet peas.

There is a shifting grace about you, in the slow way you walk, in the way you keep your eyes down, as though the ground may give way any minute.

You are beautiful, all the college boys said so.

I don't know what we said, except you talked about our maths class and how fast the holidays were passing. You weren't wearing any makeup, your lips were dry and brown, your hair flew about your face so sweet, sweet peas in the air.

'That girl has bad character, Bimal. She laughs with anyone, talks with anyone, goes all over Kathmandu by herself. Have you seen the way she looks at boys in class? And she's dark, she's really, really dark, Bimal, yes she's pretty but she can't be a wife. And besides, the complications, inter-caste, your father and the children would always be stigmatized. Meaning, she's not— what's her caste, that girl?'

I never spoke again to Nirmal, not sincerely that is. Of course

I did talk to him, he was my best friend, but I never told him what I really felt inside, just laughed with him and pretended to be all right. Sometimes I see him these days when I return from the store, and we both pretend not to see each other, maybe that's how friendships end: with eyes averted.

We were at Kalyan Bikram's son's wedding when he said that. We'd eaten, everyone was waiting for the groom to return with the bride except for us—we were waiting for Binita Rawal because I was supposed to look at her then and she was supposed to look at me. Things would proceed from there. The wedding band struck up one Hindi love song after another; I don't remember what was in fashion. Sometimes someone would shout, 'They're here,' and people would swarm to the gate. Then the music would end with a squawk of trumpets, and people would say, 'False alarm,' and the crowd would scatter, chattering. And Nirmal would begin about his cousin Rekha. To make him quit I said, 'She runs a cake shop.' He said, 'You don't want your wife to be more educated than you. Or earn more than you. That Binita Rawal works at the Himalayan Bank, friend. And she's MA-passed.'

I said, 'There must be a better name than Bake-Cake. Himalaya Cake Shop, anything.'

He said, 'You can't marry that low-caste girl.'

Then I asked how my suit looked and he said good, and we talked about other things, but what he'd said stayed with me: Binita Rawal was more educated than me, and she would probably always earn more. And she had a long face and she'd had a boyfriend. It was lucky that she didn't come to the wedding by nine. I walked home behind my father, silent, light-footed, free as he muttered about who did they think they were, weren't we good enough, didn't they know how respectable rich admired from all quarters he was in this city.

What do you think, Lalita, the thirty-two attributes of the perfect Hindu woman are? We always hear, don't we, of the thirty-two attributes, the thirty-two attributes—we always joke about them, but what do you think they are: big eyes, fair skin, a girl who smells of sandalwood and sings like a bird, do you think, a girl who plays the sitar and knows the esoteric arts—of love, what? Women from the days of the Mahabharata. Auntie showed me a passport picture of Binita Rawal and said, 'Nice, smart-looking girl,' and I wondered, smart: is that one of the attributes of a Hindu woman? You, Lalita, perfection, more than numbers can count beyond words but turned against me, you've turned…if I told you you'd laugh, or argue, you wouldn't hear me out: what did I do to harm you so much, put bitter, bitter words in your mouth so dry and brown turned the other way?

From the passport photo auntie gave me, I could see Binita Rawal had a long face and eyes set too far apart, that's all I could see. I didn't agree to meet her at a tea party, did I? Maybe, I thought, she doesn't want to marry me either, maybe that's why she didn't come to the wedding. Maybe I'd be her oppressor, and this way I could liberate her into her own and maybe she's still got a boyfriend she loves, who knows…anyway it turned out I loved you already.

My father began to talk about how I should marry the Rawal girl and work at his factory—'You wouldn't want your wife to support you'—and I decided that was the last time I'd talk to him and it was, in a way it was.

Do you know how many times I went to New Road, circled the statue of Juddha Sumshere, looking, looking, hoping to find you the way I had the day you were buying sweet peas? My eyes skimmed the girls and my heart beat fast whenever I saw a wisp of hair that looked like yours, a lip that tilted the same slow way. Ask me the name of any cassette or video store, ask me what kind of businessmen go to lunch at Point One European Restaurant for lunch, what kind go to Curry N Kabab. I know that junction, I can still taste its grit in my mouth; the traffic policeman came to recognize me. At the corner tea shop, I lingered over stale crusts of potato patties, writing your name in hot sauce. The woman at the stove began to call me her little brother. The fat shopkeeper of Anand's Music Store next door sold me John Lennon's *Imagine* when I was looking for the Eagles's *Hotel California*, and I didn't even mind. Hordes of people I paid homage to in order to catch a glimpse of you.

'Bimal?' You stood there that spring morning like a gift from heaven, breathtaking. And you talked and I talked and we walked together down narrow Makhan alley so close till I felt giddy enough to ask you if you wanted tea. I spent the whole hundred-rupee bill that I'd taken from my father's room on two special milk teas with sugar and one plate of fried potatoes. You talked to me and made me able to talk.

I remember you said, 'I wish campus life weren't ending. Remember Bridge Design? Vaidya Sir?'

And I, 'His walking stick?'

'You were nice to him, picking him up.'

'I was the closest.'

'It was nice of you.'

How did I—I don't know—how my heart shook when I asked you at the end if you'd ever meet me again; and when you said, where? I said how about the Himalayan Restaurant with special cabins?

Your friends will tell you what kind of shirt to wear on a date, that's what your friends will do. Nirmal said, 'This one,' and threw me a white shirt. 'Clean, crisp, simple. A real man.' Raju said, 'Too boring,' and pulled out a red sports shirt with thin yellow stripes: 'Young. Risk-taking. Confident.' Nirmal said, 'Solid.' Raju said, 'Honest, real.'

But when Binita Rawal's passport picture falls out of your closet, they say, 'She's not terrible, you should have married her.'

It was Raju who shocked me, finally. When Nirmal said that I was in love with my girlfriend, Raju said, 'Who says our Bimal lord needs to marry his girlfriend?' He said, 'He doesn't have to marry her just because she's friendly, you know what that means. She's a girl, that's all, and he'll have fun, it's natural. A wife is something else, a man can wait till he's thirty, thirty-five and find a pretty, virgin girl.'

He must have known how it would be for you if I left you, what people would say. How I felt. He should have thought.

And there were difficulties already between you and me—how many times could we meet at the Himalaya Restaurant's back cabins, the tablecloth stains the same colour of, my love, your skin, without getting caught, without being seen when we were leaving, coming, by someone who'd tell someone else who'd tell your family or mine? Consequences. Each time we met you closed more into yourself, talked less, made me reach out, finger the ridges between your knuckles, make you look up by revealing more and more and more: 'I love you, Lalita. I always will.' You, always beautiful, remote. An ache in my soul, a longing for something as simple as water, say, something as quenching as cool water on a hot dry sand day. You made me talk eloquently, or at least I thought eloquent, were you already hating me inside for the stupid things I said? 'You don't even have to wear lipstick to be pretty.' Time flew around us while we stayed still; each time I looked at my watch an hour or an hour and a half had gone by.

It was sometime after that, I don't remember, when your brother opened the curtains to our cabin. Your foot stiffened against mine as we sat—just sat, what's the harm in that—across each other and he stared at me wildly, let go of the curtains, left, and that was when I decided.

You whispered, wide-eyed, 'He's going to tell.'

I decided we should marry.

You said no: people would hate you, say you want things, wealth, upper class, higher caste, my father's money. I said it didn't matter what people...and it doesn't, does it, does it? You fell more and more silent—why? I took your silence for consent. I made all our plans in that shabby, curtained-off cabin: we'd rent a place, and I'd work at my uncle's gift shop till I found work as an engineer; you could work too, if you wanted, or you could be a housewife. I took your hands, so bony, so small, so cold, coarse and hard.

You say it's a mistake now, you were bored, you wanted some fun. Being married to me is your punishment. But we gave up our families, friends, society, tradition to forge a modern new life, a life based on love. There's no way to correct a mistake so big.

In This World As Hard As a Betel Nut

~

The number-one hit song at the time—broadcast ad nauseum on all the FM stations—was 'Betel nut', a duet composed by BB 'Be Be' Khatri. It began with lyrics sung by a man: 'He-e-ey, my love, won't you elope with me, let's set ourselves free, from society, in this world as hard as a betel nut.'

To this a woman would respond, 'He-e-ey, my love, I won't elope with you, people will talk, and I won't be able to walk, anywhere, in this world as hard as a betel nut.'

The man would repeat his plea: 'He-e-ey, my love, if you elope with me, I'll give you jewellery, you'll look so pretty, in this world as hard as a betel nut.'

'He-e-y my love, who needs jewellery, when they can be esteemed by society, in this world as hard as a betel nut.'

Happily for the man, the woman would relent to him after eight more pleas. Be Be's hit song ended with the two lovers running off amid a volley of drumbeats.

Some people said that Omnath Tripathi wasn't really a poet. This, because he hadn't published a single verse in years. How could he? He had been busy working up to under-secretary level, which he had finally reached now that his party had come to power. After all, it was Omnath's position at the Ministry of Youth, Sports and Culture, and not his poetry, that had earned him this top-floor office. There was even a waiting room outside: the under-secretary before him had only had a single room. His own room faced south, and had a large window through which it received a broad beam of sunlight on cold winter days, when the morning fog finally lifted.

It hadn't yet lifted today. Omnath, sitting with his feet against the metal grill of a heater, stared mournfully at the silvery haze outside. A vague blocky pattern sometimes emerged through the mist. This city shrouded, he thought. Its characters like spectres, disappearing into the fog and appearing again, bodies of mist misty, misty bodies of fog. A being shrouded in mist, voices in the mist. A symbol, an image, a metaphor on the mist. He pressed his toes to the warmth of the heater and turned away from the window. Why was it that he could feel so deeply, but couldn't jot his feelings down on paper? He should keep a diary, he thought. He noticed a water spot on the ceiling. It had vague yellow rings like an ancient map. A map, Omnath thought, a water map to guide characters lost in the fog...

He might have pursued this thought to see if it led below his psyche's depths to a line or two, but he wasn't alone in the room. The singer BB Khatri had arrived a short while ago and was sitting across him on the sofa, telling him about a new melody he'd just composed. 'It begins slowly,' the singer was explaining earnestly, 'then breaks into a dhin-tang of drums.'

BB Khatri looked, in Omnath's opinion, like one of his tape-cover pictures come to life. It was too picturesque, his oval, well-fed face, it made him look like—well, a man vain enough, vapid enough to call himself Be Be. Be, be what? The singer's lips were curled into the kind of wry, captivating smile that women were supposed to indulge and men to feel camaraderie with. He was wearing a red vest beneath a black leather coat, and on his feet were new-looking cowboy boots. With spurs, Omnath observed. He himself, dressed in a Chinese wool suit and formal shoes, presented a dignified, governmental air. He was content to look like the bureaucrat he had become, a man of slow gestures and intelligent features, with a tired sheen in his heavy-lidded eyes. It was only his hair, a white tangle that swept turbulently on to his forehead, which suggested that some unpredictable artistic moodiness lurked inside him, ready to emerge when inspired.

'Then the song dips a little,' BB Khatri said, lowering his gold-ringed hands to mimic the lowering of the tune. 'And goes ho-o-o-o.'

Omnath wished the singer would just say what he wanted, and leave. He obviously wanted something from him. Everybody did.

'And then,' BB Khatri said, 'drums: dhin-tang, dhin-tang, dhin-tang-tang.'

Stifling a sigh, Omnath turned back to the fog outside. The temple at the far corner of the street had barely come into view, and the outlines of its pagoda roof were shimmering in the gloom. At a shop beside the temple was a gathering of silver, ghost-like men huddled together, drinking tea. Hot tea evaporating mist, mist rising, mingling, commingling with their breaths, the spectre of their bodies the fog. Voices commingling bodies voices of fog. As Omnath looked on, the figures faded slowly, covered by a swirl of mist. He shuddered, and pressed his toes closer to the heater, to take some warmth from it.

BB Khatri was saying something else now. His tone had changed. Omnath turned to him with a start.

'I haven't been able to write any lyrics, though.' The singer's comely features were strained by a delicate frown. 'The words just won't come. Perhaps I'm getting old. Perhaps—perhaps, it's, well,' he sighed, 'this place. The chaos, the confusion, the pollution on the streets, Lord god! And the noise! Cars, buses honking teent-teent and toont-toont day and night. The dirt! And everywhere around us, poverty.' He raised his bejewelled hands as if defeated by it all.

Omnath murmured, 'Yes, it's difficult to create in these conditions.' He wondered if the singer would understand, from his tone, that it was visitors like him who crowded his mental space, hampered his—talent. It was visitors like him who had sapped him of his creativity.

But BB Khatri was as self-absorbed as he looked. 'My father, the other day,' he was now saying, 'paid sixty rupees for a dose of antibiotics. Sixty rupees! Where is the money? How can we afford? And how,' he spoke in an overly emotive style, 'how can I, seeing all this, write songs? Birds, flowers, mountains: where is the inspiration?'

Omnath's irritation flared up. 'But even in chaos, there is, isn't there, inspiration?'

'What inspiration, where?' BB Khatri said. 'I don't see. Only suffering, pain—and who wants to hear about that? And get more depressed than they already are!' He pursed his lips.

'Pollution, poverty, corruption everywhere, it robs a man of his spirit. If I may say so, Secretaryji, I don't even think I can write my own lyrics any more. I'm thinking I must ask—someone else—to write them.'

Omnath took in this unexpected turn in the conversation. This was what the singer had come for, then, to make this request. He pressed his feet into the heater. Not that he was one to write pop lyrics. But still, the thought pleased him. No one ever asked him to do things like this; it was as though they didn't think him capable. Flattered, he mumbled, 'A number-one pop singer like you.' Called Be Be, he reminded himself. The pop singer Be Be singing songs written by Omnath Tripathi? The coupling was—not entirely implausible.

BB Khatri was looking down at his hands, touched, it seemed, by Omnath's praise.

Yes, it was not implausible. 'Perhaps what is needed,' Omnath said, suddenly feeling like a mentor to this young man, who was ill-equipped for art, and likely to cave in to crass commercial temptations, 'are serious lyrics, not depressing ones, but honest ones that express the—the mood of the times. No girls as beautiful as flowers, no love songs. The time for love songs is gone I sometimes think. What we need are ballads about modern-day Nepal, modern-day life in this nation. Actually,' he said, gesturing at a neat pile of paper stacked on his desk, 'I was just beginning a poem when you arrived.' These words had a clean, honest ring to them. 'I was writing about our countrymen hiding from each other behind a veil of fog, their spirits, their souls commingling with mist, getting lost, you see, getting lost because they have only water-spot maps to guide them.'

He sat back, imagining a ballad, a tender, mournful elegy sung to the tune of a fiddle.

BB Khatri's face had taken on a perfectly blank expression.

Omnath pushed back a white shock of hair that had fallen into his eyes.

For a while the two men looked at each other in silence.

BB Khatri finally sat forward. 'So I was wondering,' he said. 'I mean everyone says—well, a man like you. Such power, such prestige, such connections. And the writer of such poems. I have a collection of yours. The first one, I think. Or the second.'

'The epic? Or the haikus?'

'I just remember one poem—it was about a waterfall.'

'A waterfall?'

'I read it, and I thought: ah, genius.'

'You're too kind,' Omnath demurred, wondering which waterfall poem this was.

'So I was wondering. I was wondering'—BB Khatri's voice dropped—'if you could help me get an American visa.'

Seventeen-year-old Kumar Lama had entered the waiting room outside the office, only to be told that Omnath Tripathi was busy. 'What kind of busy?' he asked the assistant, a bony man whose thick eyebrows joined in a V above his nose. 'Busy, busy, or does he have time to meet?'

'There's a visitor,' the man said. He was perched at the edge of a green vinyl sofa in the middle of the waiting room, shivering in his thin suit and pink muffler. He spoke with quick, clipped words: 'The pop singer Be Be's visiting.'

'How long will it take?' Kumar asked unhappily.

'No idea.' The man buried his face into his muffler.

Kumar turned to leave.

'You should wait,' the man said through his muffler.

Kumar turned back.

'It might not be much longer,' the man said.

So Kumar waited. He didn't actually have to get to the campus until midday, and he didn't want to come back here day after day for who knows how many days. Besides there was no one else waiting, and as long as someone else important didn't arrive, he'd be the first to meet the under-secretary. He asked the assistant, 'Be Be won't take long, then?'

'These important people. It could take several hours.'

Kumar frowned. 'Shouldn't you know?'

The V of the man's eyebrows flattened, and he lifted his face out of the muffler, grinning. 'What makes you think I'd know? Do you think I'm his assistant?'

Kumar flushed deeply. How stupid of him. Of course—the man's knees stuck out, all bones, and he wore Indian shoes, no socks. He was just a villager of some sort, here to beg the under-secretary for some favour.

Ignoring the man's grin, he went across the room and sat on a wooden bench, far enough so he wouldn't have to continue the conversation. With a deliberate show of unconcern he studied a framed photograph of Mount Everest hanging on the walls. Beside it was a Japan Airlines calendar flipped to May of last year. Japan: Kumar looked more closely. The fact that the picture had orange blossoms struck him as somehow auspicious. He studied the rest of the room. In the far corner of the room were shelves crammed with official leaflets about Nepal's rich cultural heritage. A Seiko clock above the door showed a quarter past ten.

The man seemed eager to talk. 'You want him to fix you a visa?'

Kumar smoothed a crease in his corduroy pants.

'Japan visa?' he persisted. 'Or America? Yes: a student like you—in college, am I right—would prefer America.'

Kumar asked, 'Are *you* waiting for a Japan visa?'

The man shook his head no.

'Korea?'

'I'm trying for Kuwait. To work as a gardener. Our under-secretary said he could arrange it.'

Kumar asked, 'How much did you have to pay him?'

To this, the man just said, 'Money, money,' and stared at Kumar with a purse of his lips.

What an erratic man this was. Kumar turned back to the Japan Airlines calendar. May: a picture of white blossoms in a square wooden vase. There were pipe factories in Osaka that needed workers, he had heard. Word had it the under-secretary charged forty thousand to arrange Japan, maybe less for Seoul.

The two of them sat in uneasy silence.

Then the man started up again. 'Waiting, waiting, waiting,' he said. 'Waiting, waiting.'

Slightly unnerved, Kumar asked, 'How long have you been waiting?'

'Waiting.'

'Me, I'm not in a hurry,' Kumar said. 'But some people, isn't that so, are.'

At this the man shot up from the sofa and began to pace

about with quick, springy steps. 'Are some people in a hurry?' he said. 'I don't know. How would I know? I wait all day.' Catching the window's light, his eyes glinted. 'I'm a doorman, you see. And what kind of a hurry is a doorman in? No kind of hurry at all.' He reached the room's far corner and spun around, fixing a gleaming gaze upon Kumar. 'Do you know, I even read Omnath Tripathi's poems to show that I admired him. Or tried to, tried to.' He grinned. 'There was one poem called "The Fragrance of Jasmine". It said the fragrance of jasmine is sweet. But who doesn't know that the fragrance of jasmine is sweet? You know and I know. The fragrance of jasmine is sweet. The poem was two-three lines. Did I need to read it to learn that the fragrance of jasmine is sweet?'

Kumar smiled to placate him.

But the man seemed gripped by irritation. 'So finally,' he said, 'there was no option but to join our under-secretary's party. How can he refuse a favour to a party member? That's what I figured. Are you in the party too?'

'No,' Kumar said, hoping to end the conversation. This man—who as it turned out was just a doorman—was a most disagreeable fellow.

But the man continued. 'People like us,' he said, approaching Kumar, 'we have to wait for everything.' He stopped within a foot of him, which was closer than Kumar preferred. 'But you, the son of a merchant—your father must have some land in the village.'

'Everyone has some land in the village,' Kumar said.

'And you're going to, aren't you, make him sell it to send you to America?'

Kumar shifted on his bench. 'Japan.'

The man smirked.

It irked Kumar. 'So what if my parents sell some land?' he said.

'Exactly.' With a sudden, swift move, the man lunged forward and lifted his hand and Kumar shrank back, but it turned out that the man was only taking off his pink muffler. He folded the cloth and wound it once again snugly around his neck. Kumar kept an eye on him.

When the man finished knotting his muffler, he looked up and held out a dark, bony hand.

Kumar shook it cautiously.

'I'm Naresh. My shift begins at eleven. I have to go. We'll meet again tomorrow.'

Kumar's heart dropped. 'Dai,' he said, addressing the man as an older brother. 'You don't think I'll get to meet the under-secretary today?'

With a sweetness that sounded perfectly sincere, Naresh said, 'I truly hope you do, Bhai.'

When he slipped out of the room, Kumar felt abandoned. Forlorn, he stood and went up to the Japan Airlines calendar. May. The blossoms were beautiful. That square vase was nice. Orange blossoms: found in Japan, and also found in Kumar's village, small and white and fragrant in the fall.

If he had to go back there, he would die.

He began to pace the room, one side to the other. He was too educated to go back to the village and too poorly connected to find work in Kathmandu. And he wasn't being unrealistic; he wasn't aiming for America. No: Osaka—if not, Seoul. At any cost. He would wait as long as he had to.

If there was a god of orange blossoms, please let him grant him a visa, Kumar prayed. He stopped at the door to the under-secretary's office and leaned into its buckled plywood surface. Some muffled voices echoed beyond, but he couldn't make out the words.

The Seiko clock showed ten to eleven. Kumar was getting cold. He perched on the green vinyl sofa, shivering slightly, attending the door.

The under-secretary of the Ministry of Youth, Sports and Culture, inside, was telling Be Be why it was impossible to honour his request. 'The American embassy does not accept bribes,' he said, speaking slowly, with exaggerated civility. 'The old counsellor was transferred last year, as you may have heard. He and I had connections… But that is not the main problem. The main problem is that I, you see, do not do that kind of work. This is the main problem.'

Though he looked callow, Be Be was gifted at reading people. Personal relations were the essence of existence, he felt in his more philosophical moments. Personal relations were what made people exist, or be. Or: be, be. 'Of course I can pay my way,' he said in an easy, moneyed tone. 'It's just that my application's already been rejected once…'

'Rejected once!' The under-secretary seemed oddly elated to hear this. A sweep of hair unloosed on to his forehead as he sat forward. 'Once rejected, always rejected. That's the embassy's policy, you see. That's why I say it's better not to have applied than to have applied and been rejected. This is what I say. It's better for a man not to have applied.'

Tilled Earth

Be Be smiled to disguise his irritation. How much was the under-secretary angling for? He was quite confident that he could meet the man's price. People like this—with literary pretensions—just had bigger egos, they bargained hard. Be Be patted his leather jacket into place, straightened his red vest and murmured, 'But with your connections, Secretaryji.' Then he placed his hands on his cheeks in such a way that made his gold rings glitter. 'Because money is no obstacle for someone like me, who's been blessed, thank the gods, with popular affection. People seem to like my songs, who knows why…'

The under-secretary broke in, 'Because they lie.'

Be Be stopped smiling, taken aback.

'You lie about the world we're living in,' the under-secretary said, his voice rasping. He leaned so far forward that he almost slipped off his chair. 'They don't tell them the truth, that the country is in a crisis, that the world is going badly. They go on about the mountains, the streams, love, love, love. You lie, you outright lie in your songs.'

'Well anyhow,' Be Be said, forcing another smile. 'Now tell me, Secretaryji, what I can do'—and here he measured his words— 'to enable you to arrange me this visa.'

The under-secretary snarled, 'Do you take me for a cheap middleman?'

Be Be feigned hurt. 'Now, Secretaryji!' He took a pleading tone. 'It's very important to me. Very important. And I'm willing to do anything…'

The under-secretary suddenly sat back, looking exhausted. 'It's true, I used to arrange visas, it's true.' He said, 'It's true.' The circles beneath his eyes had come into prominence. 'But

I've stopped,' he said. For a while he stared hard at the stained wall across the corner. When he spoke again, his voice was hoarse. 'I'm listening to an inner voice, you know, a calling. Saying write. Write, finally write. Write something, write something good. About beings, you see, misty beings fading, vanishing, then appearing in this city of ours.' He turned away from the singer, towards the shrouded city, and said, 'I'm writing, I have to write. I. Omnath Tripathi. Fixing visas. No.'

Be Be frowned. How much was he angling for? Fifty thousand? Sixty thousand?

'No,' the under-secretary repeated.

Seventy thousand? Be Be kept trying to read the man's expression.

On the main tourist avenue, Naresh Pariyar arrived at the Hotel de Himalayan Shangrila, changed into his uniform, and came to stand at attention by the heavy glass doors, looking his usual joker self: a man with sharp Hindu features dressed in Sherpa robes and red wool boots. Not that the hotel guests noticed how wrong it all was. A Nepali was a Nepali to tourists.

Naresh was feeling elated today for no discernible reason. Perhaps it was the quality of the light: the morning fog had finally lifted, and a faint, cool sun was just beginning to glimmer in the sky. The coldest days of winter had passed.

Or perhaps it was the realization that he had come to recently: there is life, just life, the grit of it, that's all. This thought had come to him a few days back. Like a flash. It clarified everything. When he shared this insight with his wife, she had agreed: it's all grit, this life of the poor, it's all grit.

Three children to raise somehow, while Kuwait blinked and wavered like a trick of the eye. Sometimes it made Naresh so desperate he wanted to become a child again, a child at play. Because play he could, couldn't he, despite being a nobody, play he could. He thought back to the college boy who had come to meet the under-secretary today—his soft, cold-creamed look. An educated boy claiming to have big problems. What a laugh!

Naresh grinned to himself, stretching his back, offering his thin chest to the glimmering sunlight, trying to receive warmth from it. Enjoyment. One had to savour each rare pleasure life offered.

'He-e-ey my love,' he started to hum to himself, but he stopped mid-breath when he saw, from across the glass doors, a Dutch man who had arrived two nights ago. The man had tipped him five rupees after he had carried his bags into the lobby. At the time he had felt humiliated by the sum. Now he found this funny. A man spends hundreds and thousands of rupees to come all the way from Holland, and tips a doorman five rupees.

Tourists. What a laugh! As the man approached, Naresh pulled open the heavy glass doors. Then, doffing his fake Sherpa cap, he bowed deeply to make an ostentatious display of his servility.

The Student in Love

~

Nirmal Bhattarai walked past the bridge, clambered over the fence and skirted a heap of refuse at the crossroads. In twenty minutes he reached the campus road. There he spotted his best friend, and ducked into an alley. He was in no mood for small talk. His neck was hot and his mouth parched, so he stopped awhile at the foot of a bottlebrush tree. The morning was torrid, but the shade of the bottlebrush was touched by almost-cool winds. Nirmal felt drained by the walk. He waited till a bit of energy stirred inside him. Starting off, he soon passed the taxi stand and fenced-off ping-pong club. Boys were idling there because it was too hot to play. On the next block, hordes of men came streaming out of the movie hall. Nirmal, shoving against them, felt a great urge to slide his lover's thighs against his own.

It was almost ten o'clock when he reached the girls' hostel. He found Meena's door padlocked from outside. He faltered. Yes. She had classes this morning. Now he remembered.

There was a sound behind him and he turned to see the children from the school next door tiptoeing into the yard to steal buds from the apricot tree. One of them saw him and froze. Then the others also saw him, and they all fled, squealing.

'Stealing flowers!' Nirmal shouted after them. 'I'll teach you, for stealing flowers!'

But he could not be bothered to chase after them. Instead he went up to the apricot tree, and fingered a silken white bud. It would be hours before Meena got back from classes. He ran a hand along the tree trunk. There was no point in waiting here. But it was too hot to walk all the way home. He had no money for bus fare.

So Nirmal sat in the shade of the apricot tree and, lulled by the heat, fell asleep.

The Hungry Statistician

~

The five most widely farmed grains of the nation are paddy maize wheat barley millet.

Paddy maize wheat barley millet.

Paddy maize wheat barley millet.

Paddy maize paddy maize wheat barley paddy maize wheat barley wheat barley millet.

As soon as I finish this report I'll go eat some paddy maize wheat barley millet.

The Buddha in the Earth-Touching
Posture

~

I have always thought of myself as a Buddhist. I despise empty rituals and—since my youth—have remained agnostic on the question of god. The simple life appeals to me and I have always been intrigued by the notion of extinguishing desire. A quiet wisdom infuses me when I think: life is dukkha, suffering. I want to learn how to be at peace. And since retirement I have been fortunate enough to seek out the Buddha's teachings.

I am lucky in other ways as well. I have been able to lead a comfortable life even as my country has got mired in war. Of course one cannot stay wholly impervious to the sorrows of others. The massacre of King Birendra heralded greater calamities for the nation. Why blame only one side? Between the Maoists and the army, there has been unforgivable bloodshed, and kidnapping, torture, disappearance. There are blockades, bans, closures all the time. I worry for my children's generation: their future is anxious. I, though, have been able to lead my life in dignity. It has long been my dream to learn about the dharma, as I have been able to since last year. I have even taught myself the practice of mindful breathing. After all, this late stage of life is meant for inner quests.

It was in the spirit of such a quest that I visited the Buddha's birthplace, Lumbini, some months ago. I had to lie to my wife and tell her I was attending a conference there. I feared she would accompany me otherwise. She is a person driven by passion, the kind who supplicates to every god; to her the Buddha is merely an avatar of Vishnu. While I look upon him as a sage, a wise man. A historical figure. There is a disparity of vision. Also, I wanted to be alone, or needed to.

The flight from Kathmandu to Bhairahava takes only thirty-five minutes. Looking out of the Twin Otter, I saw the Himalayas gleaming above the smog level, and felt a tingle of anticipation. I used to travel seven, eight times a year—within the country, but also on foreign tours. I went to New York, Brussels, Beijing and Islamabad in my last year in service alone. Since retirement, naturally, I hadn't had occasion to go abroad, or even outside Kathmandu. I realized, on that flight, how I had missed travelling.

Soon enough we lowered into the smog, and landed with a bump at Bhairahava's airport. I had come here two years ago, accompanying the minister. Then of course the ministry cars had all been waiting to receive us. This time I had to hire a taxi from the nearby stand, which was easy enough. Soon the driver and I were off, speeding along the highway. I enjoyed the rush of air from the open window. The winter crops had been planted, but were yet to sprout. Every now and then we passed by dense outgrowths of mustard and pulse.

'On a pilgrimage, sah'b?' the driver asked.

'No.'

I feel that one's faith should be a private matter. Part of the problem in Nepal—and indeed in all of South Asia—is that everyone is always declaring one's faith in public. This seems, to me, to derive from a pre-modern mindset. In Europe, America, it is rude to inquire after someone's religion. I admire such discretion.

'Which office?' the driver asked.

'What?'

'You're here on official work, sah'b?'

'No,' I said.

'You want to hire a taxi on a per day basis?'

'No. No.'

He then left me in peace.

This kind of confusion is understandable. Unlike foreigners, we Nepalis travel mostly on pilgrimage, or on work—generally, we travel only if someone pays us to. Internal tourism, or the concept of travelling within our country purely for enjoyment, is still new to us. To visit the Buddha's birthplace for pilgrimage is understandable. To do so simply for one's own edification is unusual.

I had prepared well for my journey, reading extensively on Lumbini and also packing along several books and reports to peruse during my visit. The legend of Siddhartha Gautam of course is widely known. At the time of his birth, in 642 BCE, Lumbini was a 'mind-captivating' garden at the boundaries of the Sakya and Koliya kingdoms. It is said that the Sakya queen Mayadevi, who had been born to the Koliya kingdom, was travelling, ten months pregnant, to her maternal home when she went into labour in the garden. After bathing in a pond there, the queen took the support of a saal tree and gave birth to her first child, a son. She died a week later, leaving the infant prince to her husband's care. Despite his privilege, King Suddhodhana could not shield his son from the sorrows of life: breaking the confines of the palace walls, Prince Siddhartha Gautam witnessed the suffering of being human. At the age of twenty-nine, in the secrecy of night-time, he abandoned his father's kingdom—and his sleeping wife, Yashodhara, and son, Rahul—to seek liberation.

There are other aspects of Lumbini that I find just as fascinating. Back when I started out in the civil service, His Majesty's Government entrusted Lumbini to an autonomous body called the Lumbini Development Trust. It has developed Lumbini into an international pilgrimage site, as per a United Nations master plan. I had never, in my long career, had the time to see the master-plan area. I was very curious about it.

As we neared the master-plan area, all the shops, restaurants and businesses took on Buddhist names: the Nirvana Photo Studio, the Gautam Buddha Lodge, the Mayadevi Hotel, the Lord Buddha Petrol Pump. The motivation for this was purely commercial. As in the rest of Nepal the people of the Lumbini area are overwhelmingly Hindu; though Muslims, too, live here in large numbers. This is actually part of Nepal's Muslim belt. I remembered this as we passed a small mosque with tall, attractive minarets.

I had booked myself into the Peace Rest House with the aid of the internet. Upon retirement I have made it a point to familiarize myself with computers, not wanting to fall behind the technological progress of our times. Though my younger son gets impatient with me, he has given me several lessons; and I have fiddled around independently, navigating the World

Wide Web on my own. I could not actually register in on the internet; but I got the Peace Rest House's number off a website. To my wife I had to say I would be staying at a government guest house.

The rest house, when we reached it, was adequate. The front desk attendant, a dark, fine-featured local man who spoke Nepali with a marked Avadi accent, showed me to a spare but clean room with a double cot and an attached bathroom. I had asked that there be no TV, and was glad that there was none. Sometimes the news channels are irresistible. The attendant asked if I would like a tour guide. I declined. I told him I wished to rest awhile before sightseeing. Not that sightseeing was what I had come to do.

Maybe it was the warmth of the southern climes. A certain malaise overcame me when I lay down on the cot. I read about Lumbini till the late afternoon, by which time it seemed to be too late to embark on any meaningful tour of the area. There was, in any event, time enough. I had booked my room for three nights, and could extend as I wished—explaining to my wife that the conference was running over. She is a simple person; she would not think to complain.

For some reason I was still feeling a bit tired the next morning. But after taking my morning meal in my room, I forced myself out. Sometimes there is no other way to get going.

'Guide, sah'b?' the front desk attendant asked again.

Again I declined.

I hired a bicycle-rikshaa to the main gate of the master-plan area, an arch—not so far from the rest house—bearing the banner 'Lumbini the Fountain of World Peace'. Indifferent guards waved us past. Inside, the first sight that assaulted me was of a row of buses in a parking lot. Hundreds of people were filing out of them, and heading eagerly for a line of stalls that were hawking prayer beads, scarves, flags. Naturally, I was put off. How banal people are. They come all the way here just to buy the same kitsch you can find anywhere in the rest of the country. Beyond the stalls was a very fat monk wearing sunglasses aggressively thrusting an oversize begging bowl before passers-by. Right behind him was a signboard warning of 'false monastics'.

I paid the rikshaa-wallah, picked up a Lumbini Development Trust brochure at the entrance and headed to a section called the Sacred Garden. Inside, there were tidy brick ruins. I might have mistaken them for remains from the Buddha's time, but I knew from my readings that they were actually the remnants of monastic communities that had risen and fallen here from the third century BCE to the eighth century CE. Government archaeologists had unearthed them in 1933, in an amateurish stab at excavation that had amounted to a quite unprofessional raze. In the 1970s His Majesty's Government had reconstructed the ruins; but because the bricks had not been placed back by date, they were merely of decorative value now.

I was displeased to see that this information was not available in the brochure. The Sacred Garden was described instead as a 'timeless place' with a 'serene spiritual atmosphere'. I would have preferred a frank discussion on the science—and guesswork—that has gone into identifying this site as ancient Lumbini. I knew a little bit about this:

I believe that the first descriptions of the 'Lum Min' grove were found in the diary of a Chinese monk, Fa Hian, who had visited the Buddha's birthplace in 409 CE. Another Chinese monk, Huan Tsang, had also written of his pilgrimage to the 'La Fa Ni' gardens in the seventh century. In later centuries, pilgrims had continued to visit the Buddha's birthplace; but by the time British explorers at the Asiatic Society—set up in Calcutta around the 1780s to 'correct the geography of Asia by new observations and discoveries'—took an interest in it, the practice of Buddhism had waned here, and the knowledge of Lumbini's whereabouts had been lost.

Nepal had then just formed as a nation. Our founding king, Prithvi Narayan Shah of Gorkha, had conquered scores of fiefdoms across the Himalayan belt, crowning his victories with the conquest of Kathmandu valley in 1767. As a staunchly Hindu king—one rightly wary of British encroachment—his first act had been to expel all foreigners from his kingdom. He refused to host the Asiatic Society's explorers on his soil.

The rediscovery of Lumbini, therefore, began more than a century later, in 1893, when the tribals of Nigliva village, north of today's Sacred Garden, led a Nepali army major to a sandstone pillar in the forests. The pillar bore an illegible inscription. By this time the pro-British Rana dynasty had usurped power from the Shah kings. They appealed to the British for help; and the Archaeological Surveyor based in Lucknow, a Viennese man named Dr Alois Fuhrer, came to inspect the pillar. He established that it had been erected in the third century by the then emperor Ashoka Maurya, a Buddhist convert said to have erected 84,000 Buddhist shrines over his empire.

Eventually, the Archaeological Survey identified this pillar as the same one that had been described by the Chinese monks. This meant that ancient Lumbini lay somewhere close by. Soon, two competing digs were under way: one, led by two Britishers, in Bihar, and another, led by Dr Alois Fuhrer, in Nepal, close to Nigliva.

But it was our own General Khadka Sumshere Rana who rediscovered Lumbini. Another sandstone pillar, in a village called Rummendei, had come to his attention. Upon investigation the general discovered that it too had been erected by the emperor Ashoka Maurya. An inscription on the pillar read:

> Twenty years after his coronation, King Priyadarsi (Ashoka), Beloved of the gods, visited this site in person and offered homage here because the Buddha, the sage of the Sakyas, was born here. He had a stone wall built around the site, and erected this stone pillar to commemorate his visit. Because the Lord Buddha was born here, he exempted the village of Lumbini from taxes and made it subject to pay only one-eighth of its produce as land revenue.

'Rummendei', it turned out, was a bastardization of ancient 'Lumbini'. And thus the Buddha's birthplace was rediscovered.

I could not see why this information had not been printed on the brochure, or posted on a signboard in the Sacred Garden. It is of vital importance that we disseminate such knowledge. For across the border, the Indians are claiming another site on their soil to be the authentic Lumbini. Nepal must forcefully counter this. After all, the Indians already have Bodh Gaya (where the Buddha attained enlightenment), Sarnath (where he gave his first teaching), Rajagriha and Sravasti (where he lived much of his life), and Kushinagar (where he died). Why give them Lumbini as well?

Disquieted by such thoughts, I made my way to the pillar discovered by General Khadka Sumshere Rana. It was a tapered phallus curtained off by a fence, and held together (for it was cracked at discovery) by two tinny bands. To my surprise I saw some visitors bowing to it. Did they think it a Shiva lingam? The pillar was not imposing to look at: its capital had fallen off centuries ago, and its original height had halved over time. There was a scrawl along the top to the order of Om Mani Padme Hung Long Live Ripu Malla, placed in 1312 by Ripu Malla, then the king of what is now west Nepal. The Brahmi inscription placed by Emperor Ashoka Maurya was below. A translation of it was propped up on a tin board beside it.

From the pillar I walked to a nearby pond. A sign declared: 'Sacred Pond: Mayadevi bathed here before giving birth to Buddha'. This, I must say, dismayed me slightly, as it was mere legend that she had bathed. One must not confuse the myth for the reality. I am not arguing with the legend, of course. I am simply saying that even if the queen had bathed, how had it been established that she had done so in this very pond?

A bodhi tree was towering over the pond, prayer flags fluttering along its branches, its trunk reddened by the vermilion that devotees had smeared on it. There is too much devotion, bhakti, and too little rationality in the way we Nepalis approach religion.

Siddhartha Gautam is said to have attained enlightenment beneath a bodhi tree, but it was a saal tree that Queen Mayadevi is said to have held on to while giving birth to her son. All right, visitors to the Sacred Garden were prone to confuse the two; the presence of a bodhi tree here was genuinely misleading. But for me, the tree raised quite another issue. The issue was: why did people pray before trees at all?

I turned away in distaste, and made my way to the Mayadevi Temple. The pride of place in the Sacred Garden had been given to this building, yet from the first glimpse of it I experienced disappointment. For the Mayadevi Temple looked like a military barracks, with its blinding white walls, gap-toothed windows, concrete stairs and pipe-lined balconies. From the roof rose a stupa of squashed proportions, with the all-seeing eyes of the Buddha looking out with an expression of surrender.

The building was in reality not a temple at all, but a shell for the remnants of a third-century Mayadevi Temple that had been excavated back in 1899. There was a damp, mossy smell to the cavernous interior. I circled a wooden walkway to reach a red sandstone frieze that depicted a voluptuously contoured Queen Mayadevi holding on to a saal tree. The newborn Siddhartha Gautam was also shown, as were the Hindu deities Brahma and Indra—by legend, these deities had witnessed the divine birth. There was also a female attendant helping Queen Mayadevi. That was her sister Prajapati, who, as legend has it, went on to marry King Suddhodhana and to raise Siddhartha Gautam alongside her own two children.

Of course no explanation about the frieze was offered anywhere. Devotees had again smeared vermilion below the frieze.

Nearby lay a triangular stone encased in bulletproof glass. I turned to this. The brochure claimed that the stone marked the exact spot where Siddhartha Gautam had been born. Based on what evidence had this claim been made? I, like anyone, enjoy a dramatic story. But, again, I would want to know if it were fiction or fact.

I regretted that a site as important as the Buddha's birthplace had been managed so casually. We Nepalis can do so much better, I thought. We must. I was standing there absorbed in this thought when two middle-aged women pressed by me. Their behaviour was typical. First they examined the frieze, then bowed down before it. Then they examined the stone, and scattered flower offerings atop its bulletproof casing. They pressed by me again on their way out.

For a moment I wondered if I were being too much of a sceptic. I turned to the brochure. It said that the newborn Siddhartha Gautam had taken seven steps and declared: 'Among all creatures I am the first and foremost to cross the riddle of the ocean of existence. I have come to the world to show the path of emancipation. This is my last birth and hereafter I will not be born again.'

No, I cannot accept such mystification.

Outside, visitors had filled a rose garden on the Sacred Garden's northern side. I was gratified to see that most were Nepali—families on day outings, student groups on school and college tours. It is important that we learn to take pride in our heritage. The few foreign tourists were looking hushed and reverent. There is a great potential to turn Lumbini into a profitable venture. Thousands of tourists already flock here, and if the proper infrastructure is put in place, thousands more could be lured.

But tourists will not come if the settings are shoddy, inferior. All the rubble from the 1933 excavation—the amateur raze—had been gathered into a mound near the rose garden, I saw. Above it sat two squat plastic water tanks. The Ministry of Science and Technology's Water and Weather Department had also set up a weather station there, in a barbed wire fence. Could they not find a more suitable place? And worse—there was a joint army and police post in the Sacred Garden. From there armed guards marched out on patrol, toting light machine guns and M16s.

It pains me to witness such negligence. It may sound immodest to say that I was one of the most competent secretaries of my time, but it is true. One lone public servant cannot of course overcome the many obstacles to good governance in a country such as ours. But I always overcame obstacles I encountered in my own postings.

My secret has been my sense of discipline. I am not especially gifted, but I maintain exacting standards for myself and for my colleagues and juniors as well. Of course there have been many highs and lows in my long career, but by the time I landed my final posting at the Ministry of Local Development—having weathered several ministers, governments and even regimes—I knew well how to transform the scattiest whims of my ministers into sound programmes and policies. There was no far-fetched dream or campaign promise that I could not translate into a feasible project or development plan.

I say all this to make the point that it should not be so

difficult to manage Lumbini properly. What seemed missing, though, was the discipline, the will.

As my rest house was not far, I decided to walk back, taking a small detour to see a sight billed by the brochure as a 'Peace Flame'. This turned out to be a fire burning dimly on a lotus-shaped stone. A sign informed me that the flame had been brought in 1986, the International Year of Peace, from the United Nations—'(New York, U.S.A.)'—in order to 'integrate peace and harmony among the globle community'. As I was leaving the Peace Flame a bus rumbled past me, kicking up so much dust that I had to cover my mouth and nose. A local tractor followed, spewing exhaust fumes. And I thought: what peace? A crane lay in disuse to one side of the road, a digger to the other. All along the path was a thicket of signboards directing visitors to the remaining sections of the master-plan area: To East Monastic Zone, To West Monastic Zone, Lumbini the Source of World Peace, Do not Enter.

It seems that one never thinks that one will grow old and fall out of use, just as one never thinks that one will one day die. In hindsight I am surprised that I did not plan my retirement. I assumed that with all my free time I could always take a week or two out, mull over my next move, design a new life project. There were so many things I had never had the opportunity to do. I could not imagine that I would not get around to them.

What I had not expected was that I would feel so—disturbed—by my domestic situation. My marital life has not been atypical. My wife and I have shared the usual joys and given each other the usual sorrows, and we have settled into a passionless partnership. Though she would never admit it, she probably likes the life I have given her more than the person I am. I do not mind this. I too find her company limited. We are not intellectual equals, merely co-owners of lives jointly led. We consult on matters relating to our sons, our house, our properties, but we do not share a joint vision.

When I stopped leaving for the office every morning, a certain tension developed between us. My presence in the house seemed to needle my wife. She was always suggesting, 'Why not visit some friends?' or 'Why not visit relatives?' even though I was content to relax at home. She has always been quite domineering in her manners. She would fill the house with orders—to our sons, to the servants. I have never accepted bribes, so our house is not sizeable. Even when I confined myself to my room, I could hear her—'Get me some tea!' or 'You've missed a corner!' or 'Don't stay out late!' A few times I tried to intervene, but she got testy: 'I've run this house perfectly well all these years, you're going to start lecturing me now?'

There was a constant sense of uproar, tumult, in the house. I always felt stressed, and found myself bickering with her over petty matters—were Glucose biscuits appropriate for serving to guests, things like that. It was not becoming of me. For the first time in my life, I began to dislike my wife quite openly. If I disagreed with her on anything—which brand of tea to buy— she behaved as though I were encroaching on her life. I suppose this is why I went to Lumbini. I am capable of so much. But I was struggling every day just to maintain some respectability in my own home. It is bewildering to suddenly lose one's station, and dignity. My wife could not, it seems, brook the fact that I was now a nobody, a nobody like her.

I awoke early on my second morning in Lumbini and set to mindful breathing. I generally use two pillows to avoid pain in the kneecaps while in the lotus position. Keeping my eyes half-open, I make an effort to follow the in breath, then the out breath, repeatedly, for twenty minutes, pushing away any thoughts and distraction. This is a completely secular practice that anyone can try.

It is a hard practice, as sometimes—like that morning—my mind refuses to remain on the breath. Almost as soon as I sat on the pillows I had a thought, and it proved a powerful distraction: I should apply for a consultancy. Many secretaries have, upon retirement, taken profitable consultancies at multilateral and bilateral aid agencies. Our inside knowledge of government is invaluable to foreigners. One may also apply to international NGOs and, failing that, one might set up an NGO of one's own.

But it is best if one can obtain a consultancy at a reputable organization, an organization that commands respect, such as, say, the United Nations. I grew fidgety at this thought. Sometimes, when it grows difficult to continue my meditation, I abandon the attempt altogether. After all, the point of meditation is to recognize one's mental state, to see, for example, how the mind flits from thought to thought when it grows agitated. It became impossible for me to continue that day. I shifted out of the lotus position, and went to my bags to pick out a few books that I wanted, quite urgently, to read.

U Thant, the third secretary-general of the United Nations, may be little remembered by the wider world, but in Nepal we

The Buddha in the Earth-Touching Posture   135

recall him fondly, for it was he who initiated the idea of developing Lumbini as an international pilgrimage site. A Burmese national with a career in education, U Thant was the first Asian to hold the top position at the United Nations. He had come into office unexpectedly, after his predecessor, Dag Hammarskjold, died in a plane crash in 1961 while still in office. Among U Thant's achievements in his first term were to commit United Nations help towards the 1961 transfer of New Guinea from the Netherlands to Indonesia, to remove Soviet missiles from Cuba in 1962, to resolve the civil war in Congo in 1963, to establish peacekeeping forces in Cyprus in 1964 and to help reach the India-Pakistan ceasefire in 1965. For his success he was re-elected to a second term.

This period proved more challenging. Plagued by the United Nations's chronic lack of funds, U Thant found himself helpless to prevent the Vietnam War or to quell the growing conflict in the Middle East. In 1967, on a tour of South Asia, he visited Nepal, and—as a Buddhist—made a special pilgrimage to Lumbini. Rumour has it that upon seeing the rot and rubble at the Buddha's birthplace, he wept.

He pledged his support towards developing Lumbini. This all happened while I was still a college youth. Our nation had launched on a frenzy of development at that time. Rana rule had ended in 1950 and, after a decade of democracy, King Mahendra had taken absolute power, promising to achieve in a decade the progress other countries had achieved over centuries. The government was constructing roads, bridges, telephone links and other physical infrastructure at a furious pace. And, mimicking the Asian and African nations newly liberated from colonialism, we were searching for a modern-yet-uniquely-indigenous identity for ourselves. This we found in the image of ourselves as a Hindu nation, with a king who was an incarnation of the divine preserver, Vishnu.

Despite this Hindu bent, King Mahendra welcomed U Thant's pledge to develop Lumbini, for he saw that the Buddha, as a son of Nepali soil, could confer as much prestige upon our land as, for example, Sagarmatha: Mount Everest. There has never been much antagonism between Hinduism and Buddhism in Nepal. Most Hindus—my wife is an example of this—view Buddhism as just another branch of Hinduism. The Buddhists are too tolerant to take offence.

In 1970, around the time I joined government service, the United Nations formed a Lumbini Development Committee in New York at the request of His Majesty's Government. Its members came from Buddhist countries like Burma, Cambodia, India, Japan, Laos, Malaysia, Singapore, Sri Lanka and Thailand. The People 's Republic of China was of course missing. But the committee also included members from Afghanistan, Pakistan and Indonesia—countries where Buddhism had preceded the rise of Islam. Led by Nepal's permanent representative to the United Nations, a career bureaucrat like myself, the committee commissioned the design of a master plan by a Japanese architect named Kenzo Tange.

I discovered, through my reading, that Kenzo Tange had played a major role in Japan's post-war reconstruction. He had risen to fame after designing the Hiroshima Peace Centre in 1949, in which he fused modern materials—such as concrete—with Japanese aesthetics. Later, under the influence of abstract internationalists such as Le Corbusier, he was drawn to drier functionalist styles. His 1960 plan for Tokyo inserted bridges, man-made islands, floating parking lots and abstract superstructures into teeming urban spaces. In 1964 he settled into teaching at the Tokyo University, regularly touring to lecture at the Massachusetts Institute of Technology, Harvard University, Princeton University, Yale University. He was at the height of his career when he won the Lumbini master-plan commission.

Kenzo Tange did not visit Lumbini during the design of the master plan. Most likely, junior associates at his Tokyo-based architectural firm did the designing, while he supervised. Not surprisingly, coordination proved challenging between his architectural firm in Tokyo, the Nepali government in Kathmandu and the Lumbini Development Committee in New York. Five years, and over a million dollars, were spent on producing the Lumbini master plan.

So interesting did I find this reading, I wanted to pay a visit to the authorities at the Lumbini Development Trust. I was curious to see what Kenzo Tange's master plan had been like, to learn if it had been faithfully implemented. I did not know if the authorities would meet just anyone. But I was hoping they might recognize my name.

At the front desk of the rest house I inquired about names and numbers. The attendant said he would get back to me, and within a half hour he knocked on my room door with the mobile and landline numbers of the chief archaeologist.

'Try him on the mobile, sah'b,' he said, offering me his own mobile set. 'The Maoists bombed the telephone tower several months ago. The lines still aren't back up.'

I called the chief archaeologist, but there was no answer. I tried again, but again no answer. The attendant stood by patiently, waiting for his set to be returned to him. I tried several more times, to no avail. The attendant finally offered to send a handwritten message to the chief archaeologist's office. 'I will request him to call you on my mobile, sah'b. He must be on a field trip. I will request him to call you back.'

That evening, sure enough, the call came. I was feeling a bit low in spirit, as I had not accomplished much that day. I was regretting having spent the day in my room. When I put the set to my ear, the line was not very good. I introduced myself, and said that I was interested to learn more about the United Nations master plan.

The chief archaeologist said something, but I could not catch it.

'Could you repeat?' I said. 'Could you repeat?'

It turned out he had not caught my introduction. I repeated my interest. It turned out he was due to go on a dig the following morning. 'Are you in a hurry?' he asked through the faulty connection. 'Can it wait till I come back in two days' time?'

'That will be too late,' I said, giving him the details of my flight out.

We fixed a time for early the following morning.

The next morning, when I got to the office—off in a mango grove in the Sacred Garden—there were two other men with the chief archaeologist. Arun Gupta and Ali Ibrahim were both working for the Lumbini Development Trust, but they were quite junior. I suppose my name had not been recognized on the phone yesterday. It seemed that they had not been expecting someone as senior as I. I felt slightly awkward about this. Nevertheless, I put my request to the chief archaeologist: 'I was hoping you could tell me how much of Tange's master plan has been implemented in reality.'

The chief archaeologist respected Tange's original vision. He explained that Tange had originally wanted thirty-seven countries—those with Buddhist populations—to build monasteries in Lumbini. These monasteries weren't supposed to be large or extravagant, he said. They were only supposed to represent all the variations in the way the dharma was practised globally.

'The only problem,' he said, 'has been in the implementation.' Funding constraints and financial mismanagement had delayed work. The master plan was still unfinished, though it had originally been slated for completion in 1987. After 1990, under democracy, work had sped up. But by then Tange's original plan had been modified. Mainly, plans to develop the agricultural capacity of the surrounding villages had been scrapped. 'And instead of allowing in monasteries from thirty-seven countries, we allowed anyone, everyone, to build a monastery here,' said the chief archaeologist. 'And that was a mistake.'

He handed me a booklet, one containing a sketch of the original master plan. I thanked him, and—because I knew I was keeping him from his dig—I stood up to leave.

Just then, the Gupta fellow revealed that he had recognized me. 'Sir, weren't you in government service?'

I said yes, but I had retired.

'I thought you looked familiar. From the TV. You were awarded a medal,' he said.

'Yes. But now I am retired.'

'Someone like you immediately finds work,' he said. 'You're fortunate.'

'I suppose I am.'

'How much does the United Nations pay Nepali consultants?'

'Excuse me?'

'Do they pay by the day or by the month?'

'I do not follow.'

The chief archaeologist intervened. 'Guptaji is hoping to be hired by the UN project here when his contract with us ends next year,' he said with a laugh. 'This is all he ever asks anyone. What is the rate for Nepalis at the UN? What kind of money can a Nepali earn?'

Gupta beamed. 'This is true. Their pay is excellent.'

'There is a UN project here?' I asked.

Gupta blurted out something that sounded like 'Twerp'.

'I'm sorry?' I asked him to repeat himself.

He said, 'Tourism for Rural Poverty Alleviation Programme. TRPAP. Will you be needing to meet their staff, sir?'

I made an indeterminate gesture.

'What exactly is the thrust of your research, sir? What kinds of information are you seeking? Is there anyone you would like to talk to? Any local people? Can we set up meetings for you?' he asked.

'Oh, please don't trouble yourself,' I said. 'You are busy with your own work.'

He said, 'It will be no problem at all.'

'No, really.' I begged off. 'Now, let me not keep you from your dig.'

The chief archaeologist stood and shook hands. Then Gupta and I shook hands. As I reached over to shake hands with the Ibrahim fellow, he said, 'Sir, are you interested to include the voice of the local people in your study? To capture the lived reality? Or do you just want'—he pointed at the booklet that the chief archaeologist had given me—'to limit yourself to such reports?'

'The local people's voices are paramount,' I said, wondering what study he was talking about.

He said, 'Then you must meet the maulana of Khungai. I will arrange it, sir. I believe you are staying at the Peace Rest House?'

A certain anxiety crept up on me upon departing from the office. Had they thought I was conducting a study? Why? Had I relayed that impression somehow? I replayed the entire phone conversation in my mind, and could not see that I had posed as anything other than what I was: an ordinary man filled with curiosity about this part of his country. Still, an anxiety nagged at me.

I walked from there to the Peace Flame, hoping that the signboards nearby it would orient me. As they did not, I consulted the booklet for the sketch of the master plan. The second section, called the Monastic Zone, was divided in two by a canal. The East Zone housed monasteries of the Theravada order, while the West Zone had been set aside for monasteries of the Mahayana order.

Why the sectarian divide? All religions are marred by sectarianism. I myself could not decide: East or West? Finally I selected the East Zone—because it was smaller, and because the teachings of the Theravada school, with its emphasis on renunciation, form the basis of the teachings of the later schools. I am also more drawn to this less ritualistic path.

The road in the East Zone was broad and empty, tranquil, deserted. One or two people—locals going about their errands, riding bicycles—passed by me, but otherwise I was quite alone. The canal separating this from the west side stretched to my side. The water was muddy, but there were ducks and geese, and the weeping willows along the edge were pleasant.

The first monastery I came upon was the Myanmar Golden Temple, an unassuming, even—save for the golden roof—austere structure. I stopped at its door, uncertain as to whether entrance was allowed to visitors. I could not see anyone outside the temple, nor hear any human sound from within. Could one wear one's shoes into monasteries, or need one take them off at the door? In the end I felt it might be inappropriate for me to go in. Monasteries are not made for gawking at, after all. And I was not given to bowing before statues. I would not want to offend anyone—if indeed there was anyone inside—by sightseeing like a tourist in a place of worship.

In the same spirit I walked past the nearby Sri Lankan Monastery and the Royal Thai Monastery, the Dhammajanani Vipassana Centre of Nepal and the International Nun's Temple, and before I knew it I was through with the East Zone.

At an open, empty plot, I sat down amid a patch of reeds to rest. Two streams, the Harhawa and the Telar, meandered through the reeds, and the wind was rippling gently through a line of weeping willows. I generally mistrust teachers, lamas, holy men. So many have been exposed eventually as charlatans and poseurs. But once I went to a dharma talk by a Tibetan lama who was about the age of my youngest son. At the end of his talk he encouraged students to ask questions. One student raised his hand and asked: why do you encourage people to bow to idols, when you know they are just made of metal or stone? And the lama said, 'The idol doesn't need you to bow to it, you need that.'

From my diagram, the West Zone appeared spread out over a vast stretch, so I hired a bicycle-rikshaa. I had thought I'd start with the Burmese Panditarama Lumbini International Vipassana Meditation Centre, but when I got there its high gate was locked. So I went next door, to the stupa of a Nepali organization, the Manang Samaj. The main shrine lay below its tall dome. Entering it, I saw a gold-plated statue of the Buddha, one hand touching the earth. An elderly caretaker, who had been sweeping the floor, stopped to allow me to worship. As I approached the statue, the metal screws along its arms, neck and waist came into view. A peacock feather was jutting out of the statue's begging bowl. There was an empty bottle of Chick K Shampoo on the altar, and a donation box. The caretaker was watching. So I gave the statue a cursory namaste. Then I put twenty rupees into the donation box and left.

Nothing—save for a feeling of fraudulence—is evoked in me by going through such motions of worship. I tried to let go of this feeling as I took the bicycle-rikshaa to the Zhong Hua Buddhist Monastery, built by the Buddhist Association of China.

This monastery held great interest for me. The Buddhist Association of China was a quasi-government group that regularly denounced the Dalai Lama for heading a 'separatist group', and the Falun Gong for being an 'evil cult'. Its monastery was built in the Qing dynasty style. The main shrine had beautiful latticed woodwork, and an enormous bronze Buddha at the altar. There was a sterile, squeaky-clean quality to everything, as though it were a museum, not a shrine. A disused incense burner stood to one side. Beside it sat a young Chinese monk hunched over a textbook of beginners' Nepali.

Soon, two bearded Muslim men wandered in and began to scrutinize the architecture. They had taken off their shoes as a mark of respect. I thought I should take mine off too. Just then a suit-clad businessman marched in, boots and all, giving the shrine a breezy glance-about. Then three teenage girls trooped in and began snapping pictures of the bronze Buddha.

The Korean Dae Sung Sa Ga Monastery, next door, was still under construction. A concrete colossus, it had rows and rows of columns in a hall vast enough to seat a thousand. I was impressed by its size: I did not know that there were any monasteries of this monumental scale, even in Kathmandu. The wrought designs along the concrete edifice already gave it a commanding look.

In the rubble-strewn grounds I happened upon the engineer overseeing the site. We exchanged greetings, I remarking on the size of the monastery.

He was a friendly man, one who took great pride in his work. He had 130 labourers on this site, he said. 'All local people. Though I'm also something of a local.' He had worked, he said, for years on a nearby road project. 'And before that I worked in India.' He named an engineering company, and looked surprised that I didn't know it. 'They have offices everywhere. In India, Singapore. Before that I worked in a British road project in east Nepal.'

Over my years in public service I had dealt with innumerable engineers at the national, district and even village level. They invariably felt they were building our country, bit by bit, as— without them—none of us would have roads, taps, bridges. They knew what needed to be done to build Nepal.

I asked him how long it would take to complete the construction here.

He rubbed his thumb and fingers, in the gesture for money. 'It's all built on donations,' he said, grinning. 'When the money comes fast, we work fast. When money doesn't come...' His grin widened.

The Koreans seemed to harbour a particular fondness for Lumbini. Next to this site stood another monastery belonging to the Yong Do Society. It too was incomplete, a tangle of exposed iron rods and bricks. Plans to build yet another Korean monastery nearby had recently been cancelled.

It seemed to me as I took the bicycle-rikshaa from monastery to monastery that there was something a bit too materialistic to the way these structures were cropping up amid what had been an open stretch of land. The rikshaa rattled by the incomplete Vietnam Phat Quoc Tu Monastery, its building—a spire of scaffolding—topped by a pagoda roof with fine, wispy curlicues. The Linh Son Buddhist Temple, of French Vietnamese origins, was also under construction nearby, as was the Ladakh Drakung of India. The Sokyo monastery of Japan, also in the building stages, was a squat dome of low, understated proportions that exuded Zen restraint. Everywhere the bicycle-rikshaa went, I encountered hectic sites of digging, lifting, transporting, sawing, drilling and hammering. It was almost a relief to see a few bare plots of a Nepali and German monasteries, which had not yet got around to constructing anything.

Tiring of these construction sites, I asked the rikshaa-wallah, a dark, skinny man, if there weren't any completed monasteries I might visit. He muttered something in Avadi, turned around and took me to the Drubgyud Choeling Monastery, run by Nepali monks. I did not go in, though. At the gate, a group of boy monks were oohing and aahing over a Harley Davidson. Some hippy foreigner was straddling it, showing off to the monks.

One would expect, from monks, some rigour. All in all, the West Zone had been a disappointment. Renunciation was little in evidence here. And where was the compassion, the main teaching of the Mahayana school? As for wisdom, or insight—the Buddha's main teaching—how could it be attained in this gaudy Buddhist wonderland?

On the way back to the rest house I passed a particularly busy construction site, where hundreds of labourers were swarming about carrying planks and cement, hammering and sawing, and chipping pebbles off rocks. The monastery itself, belonging to the Tara Foundation of Germany, was almost entirely concealed by scaffolding. I asked the rikshaa-wallah to stop awhile.

The site manager was standing at the gate. He looked at me, and I looked at him, and maybe he recognized me. He smiled and nodded, and we exchanged namastes.

I asked him about the monastery, and he offered to show me around. Leading me up a wide stairway, he said that when construction was complete a stream of water would be cascading down the front portion. 'Because water is a very important element of the dharma,' he said. He stopped beneath the scaffolding and pointed at the massive red columns with gay, multicoloured woodwork. Finely crafted frescos of bodhisattvas covered the monastery's external walls. 'Only the best artists have been put to work,' he said. Inside, artisans from Kathmandu were carving statues out of wood.

The site manager's satisfaction was obvious. 'All this,' he said, sweeping an arm over the woodwork that covered an entire side of the interior, 'we have yet to finish. And the inauguration date has already been set.'

'Who will inaugurate it?' I asked.

He laughed. 'Whoever's the prime minister at that time. They come and go so fast, you can't keep track. Or maybe we'll just invite the king.'

I was not able to formulate my exact opinion on the Monastic Zone till, the next morning, I got into a conversation with the rest house attendant. He was serving me my morning meal in the room, and I told him that I had visited the monasteries the previous day. A sly smile passed over his lips. 'What did you think, sah'b?'

'They are pretty to see,' I said, neutrally.

'We go there sometimes,' he said. 'It's good for picnics. The old people and children enjoy it especially.'

'You don't go there to worship?' I asked.

'Worship,' he said with the same sly smile, 'we can do every day in our village shrines.'

Something about this remark set me thinking. After the attendant left, I consulted the booklet on the master plan, and discovered that more than twenty-four million rupees were being spent on the construction of the Tara Foundation monastery. That was above three hundred thousand American dollars. More than forty million rupees were going into the Korean Dae Sung Sa Ga Monastery. The Zhong Hua Buddhist Monastery had cost twenty million rupees. Even the modest Theravada monasteries, such as the Royal Thai Monastery and the Myanmar Golden Temple, had cost twelve and six million rupees respectively. All in all, over six billion rupees—or eighty-two million American dollars—were being spent on the monasteries of the Monastic Zone.

All this in an impoverished area. Rupandehi district had a higher than average population growth rate, but a lower than average percentage of economically active people. Over seventy-five per cent of people here relied on subsistence farming. To supplement family income, many men migrated to India or to the Gulf states in search of work, leaving an increasing number of women in charge of impoverished households. The United Nations Development Programme had ranked the district's human development index at a meagre 0.404. A rank of below 0.5 indicates short life spans, low awareness levels and desperate standards of living.

When Ali Ibrahim showed up at ten to take me to meet the maulana of Khungai, I did not hesitate to go with him. I suppose I should have clarified to him—in case he held a mistaken belief—that I was not conducting a study of any kind.

But I did not want to displease him, as he had already taken the trouble to arrange this meeting, and I was also curious by now to hear—as he had said—the voices of the local people. What did the Muslim villages think of Lumbini? I had never, through my career, had an occasion to visit a purely Muslim community. The Muslims constitute what—three per cent? four per cent?— of Nepal's population.

Khungai lay past a string of squalid, fly-infested settlements with a few tea shops, grain stores and bicycle-repair workshops of slapped-together tin sheets. We disembarked from the bicycle-rikshaa at the village mosque, and Ibrahim led me to its grassy courtyard, where schoolchildren, students at an attached madrassa, were sitting on rows of benches, facing a blackboard that had been propped up on a tree. They all turned to look at us, and stared at me the entire time I was there.

The maulana was an elderly man with a long, flowing beard. He spoke only Urdu. Ibrahim translated for us.

Solemnly, the maulana said his people had benefited from Lumbini's development as an international pilgrimage site. The government would not otherwise have built roads or brought electricity to this area. Translating for him, Ibrahim said, 'Transportation is easier now than it used to be. It used to take a full day to even reach Bhairahawa.'

I felt that the maulana was probably holding back. I asked, 'But what real benefit has there been in these villages?' I thought of the billions of rupees—millions of American dollars—being spent in the Monastic Zone. 'Are you any better off than you would have been?'

Maybe Ibrahim misunderstood the question, or mistranslated

it. 'Our people are very poor,' he said, translating the maulana's answer back to me. 'We are all farmers here, and we are all suffering, because there is no water for our fields. What we need above all are irrigation canals.'

At this point the maulana said something else. Ibrahim translated: 'Of course that is the government's job. But if the Lumbini Development Trust offered us training, we could find other forms of employment. They could also work for greater sanitation in this area. They could invest in our schools and health care.'

'Yes,' I said. 'And also the monasteries? What, really, have they done for the local people? For people such as'—I pointed at the gawping schoolchildren—'such as these.'

After some consultation between the two, Ibrahim said, 'The International Buddhist Society, an NGO, conducts free health clinics and sanitation drives. And we are also helping ourselves.' Among the Muslims, he said, there was a practice of donating 2.5 per cent of all household income towards social causes. Most families in this village donated their share to the madrassa, which educated seventy-five boys and girls till the fourth grade. Some also gave alms to the poor, or to those in difficulty. Ibrahim said that some of the better-off villages nearby had used their funds to operate health care centres and private schools. 'There's even a college campus not far off,' he said. 'All this we have done for ourselves.'

'Yes. Exactly. Now why can't the monasteries do the same?'

Both the maulana and Ibrahim hesitated.

'They are throwing so much money around,' I said. 'For what?'

The maulana smiled uncomfortably, and looked down at his hands.

'Maybe the monasteries are doing something in other villages,' Ibrahim said. 'It could be that we don't know about it. Your study,' he added, 'is it about development? Or is it about social issues?'

'Oh,' I said. 'About development.'

We spent another few minutes discussing irrigation canals.

Afterwards, on the rikshaa ride back to the hotel, I worried that I may have appeared to be baiting the maulana, urging him to speak badly of the monasteries. But my intention had not been to pit the two religions against each other. For I myself was Hindu—born to a Hindu family, that is—but I would be the first to say that the Hindu population of this area surely fared no better than the Muslims. The Chamaars—a caste traditionally considered low, as shoemakers—suffered the daily humiliation of untouchability: they could not share food, water or living space with those of the so-called 'higher' castes such as myself. Now of course, with some Dalit rights activism, the Chamaars were becoming more aware of their rights. But the only thing that can truly make them equal is wealth. Wealth is the great social leveller, I feel.

When I got back to the rest house, I found Arun Gupta waiting for me. There was another man with him, a Laxman Baniya, who worked at the United Nations project that Gupta had mentioned in our first meeting: twerp, or something like that.

Beaming, Gupta said, 'We were passing by, and thought: Sir is probably having lunch all by himself. We should give him some company.'

I had to invite them to lunch. We sat in the rest house's garden restaurant, and ordered three plates of daal-bhat: they non-vegetarian, myself vegetarian. With lunch they ordered beer. I too was tempted into doing so.

I don't know what Gupta had told him about me, but Baniya seemed to feel that he had to tell me about his work. His only grievance with Kenzo Tange's master plan, he said, was that it did not enable the local people to earn any money through tourism. He said that the third section of the master-plan area, a section I had yet to visit called the New Lumbini Village, had a low-budget Sri Lankan rest house for pilgrims, and the costlier Japanese Mikasa and Hokke hotels, which catered to richer tourists. Plans were also under way to construct cheap camping grounds, a youth hostel and accommodations for medium-budget visitors. 'And,' Baniya added, growing indignant, 'many of the monasteries also offer free lodging for pilgrims. So: how can local entrepreneurs compete? Who will stay at a hotel, as sir has done, when they can stay for free at a monastery?'

'After all,' Gupta piped in, 'not everyone has a United Nations job.'

'Indeed not,' I agreed.

Then I realized what had gone wrong.

Due to the poor phone connection when I had first called the chief archaeologist, there had been a misunderstanding: when I had asked about the 'UN master plan', I had been heard, it seems, to be claiming to have come from the United Nations.

I suddenly realized how awkward a position I was in. Gupta, Ibrahim—and the chief archaeologist—would eventually find out from the United Nations, maybe even via this Baniya fellow, that I had not come from the United Nations…

Baniya was now telling me of a hotel management committee that his project had set up. 'We've also trained local people to work as front desk staff,' he said. Indeed, he seemed to be reporting to me as a junior staff would to a senior. He said his project had also set up a tour guide association, which trained people to work as guides. The project had also set up a union for rikshaa drivers. 'We've also arranged for the hotels to buy local flowers and handicrafts,' he said, growing fairly breathless. 'And we've even encouraged local artists to mould Buddha statues out of Lumbini clay.'

I myself was growing exceedingly uncomfortable. 'Oh?'

He went on. His project had fitted several villages with water pumps and incinerators in order to improve health and hygiene of this area. He himself had helped people form savings groups; over the course of two years, sixty-seven groups had saved, altogether, 90,000 rupees. These groups would eventually take out small loans to start up enterprises such as rearing chickens or goats.

We had finished our lunch by then. I felt I had to put an end to it. 'While all this is good to hear,' I said—all the while thinking 90,000 rupees: a piddling 1,200 dollars?—'it is not related to the topic of my interest.' I stood to indicate that our lunch had ended. 'Nevertheless, I am glad to have met you.'

'Oh. Namaste, then.' Baniya stood, looking surprised.

Gupta said, 'What exactly is the topic of your study, sir?'

'The Muslims,' I said. 'I am studying the status of Muslims in Nepal.'

After a few hours in my room, succumbing to a sudden bout of malaise, I went downstairs and, using the hotel attendant's mobile, called my wife in Kathmandu to inform her that I would be back on the next day's morning flight, as scheduled.

'Aren't you ashamed?' she cried, shrilly. 'Shouldn't you have called earlier? We didn't know what had happened!'

Patiently, I explained to her that there were no landlines here, as the Maoists had bombed the telephone tower.

'The Maoists? The Maoists!'

I assured her that I was in no danger. 'The conference,' I said, 'ended early. So I have been touring the Buddha's birthplace. I am quite all right.'

'You're on a pilgrimage? You might have told me! I could have come too!'

'Another time,' I promised her. 'Another time.'

It was about four o'clock when I got through with the call. A part of me wanted to return to my room and lie in my cot, reading; but another part of me wanted to resist this lassitude. It was not healthy for a man to lie about idly.

I decided to visit the New Lumbini Zone, the section of the master-plan area that by Baniya's account had discouraged local entrepreneurship. I walked all the way. But what I saw there was unremarkable: a vast, reed-covered lot with staff quarters, a library and an auditorium. The buildings for the latter two were cylindrical in shape, and they looked peculiar, out of place, like primitive space ships. As I was turning away I spied a plaque by the auditorium door. It was a dedication. To U Thant. Upon his death in 1974. Three years after he had left the United Nations.

Suddenly my vision blurred, and a hot tear trickled down my cheek. It struck me as so sad that here, in this reed-covered expanse, amid these cylindrical buildings, began an idea that—though flawed in execution—had been pure in its original intention. It might never have happened, any of this, except for an accident of history. U Thant might never have become the United Nations secretary-general. Or he might never have visited Lumbini. Certainly, his successor Kurt Waldheim—a Nazi—would not have developed the Buddha's birthplace. Javier Perez de Cuellar, Boutros Boutros-Ghali? It was only because of U Thant. U Thant did all this. He bestowed this gift to us Nepalis, left this mark of his time on earth. It made me feel completely bereft to think: Why had he died so soon after leaving the United Nations?

I sobbed openly. I don't know how long I stood there, trying to stop. Finally, I left the cylindrical buildings and made my way to a patch of wetlands nearby. It was completely secluded there. I thought that it might help me to breathe mindfully, so I sat cross-legged on the ground and assumed the lotus position. But as soon as I tried to focus on the in and out breaths, a sudden grief threatened to overcome me, and my vision would blur. I concentrated harder, and even tried counting my breaths: one, two. One, two. But it was no use. The grief finally engulfed me, and again I sobbed.

I am competent; I work hard. There is so much that I can do yet. In this backward country where people are full of passion but have not a jot of wisdom I am reasonable, I am rational, I am a modern man. This country needs me; it needs people like me. It should be grateful that I even live here any more. How many secretaries have taken green cards and moved to America? Am I like that? Did I line my pockets when I had a chance? I have devoted all my life to serving my country and now what does my country do? Just discard me like a used rag. Just leave me to wait for my death…

It was a long time before I regained my composure; when I did so, I felt drained, exhausted. I did not know if I had the strength to walk all the way back to the rest house. I sat there, by the wetlands, looking at birds: shanks, ibises, sandpipers, water hens. This was, I discovered from a nearby signboard, a sanctuary for 130 species of birds, established by the International Union for the Conservation of Nature and the International Crane Foundation. Seeing the signboard made me feel sad again. Everyone, I thought, had a place in the world. Everyone had work to do save me.

Again a few tears sprang to my eyes.

And again, in time, I recovered.

At one point a stork flew by, and some herons came to peck at the reeds near me. As the sun lowered in the sky, a flock of egrets came to perch on a saal tree across the wetlands, their pale plumes glistening against the sky. In the wetlands I also saw a creature that I had never seen before: a blue bull. It was grazing on the grassy islands, a buffalo-like beast with a powerful chest and delicate, tapered hindquarters. Its grazing led it nearer to me slowly, slowly. When it was within ten feet of me it lifted its head and stared at me awhile, assessing me. Then it lowered its head and resumed grazing.

I spent more than an hour there, till eventually I felt all right again. I felt I could walk.

Evening had fallen by then. I made my way back to the rest house via the Peace Pagoda, a white stupa on the northern edge of the wetlands. As in the Sacred Garden, there were many visitors milling about here, some taking pictures of the stupa, others of themselves. The stupa had unfamiliar golden deities along the top, and some illegible Japanese script. I stopped at a headstone at the stupa's base, and read that such pagodas had been built all over the world by a certain Fujii Guruji upon witnessing the bombing of Hiroshima and Nagasaki. Some qualms arose in me, then dissipated. A crowd of schoolchildren brushed past me on their way to circle the stupa. I joined them.

Ta'Angzoum among the Cows

~

Ta'Angzoum knows how to balance a calf on her shoulders. Not just any calf: her calf—because it is hers despite what anyone may think or whisper as she brushes past them in the village lanes. Her calf. For it, she has set apart the entire first floor of her house, a dark, windowless stall that smells of dung and feed. She and her mother share the only other room in the house, the room above the stall, beside the narrow veranda. It is to this veranda that Ta'Angzoum must carry her calf every day. There it luxuriates in the bright high-altitude sunlight.

Ta'Angzoum now stoops under the calf and heaves it on to her shoulders. She totters under the weight of the animal, for she is herself a small-boned woman who stopped growing long before she should have. Her hands, reaching out to grasp the sides of the ladder, are cracked from too much work. Too much work: every day Ta'Angzoum either weeds the buckwheat fields or cleans blocked irrigation canals or cuts grass, gathers brush, scoops dung, coats the walls with mud, chops wood, threshes grain, weaves rugs or washes clothes. Always for someone else. Ta'Angzoum's hands are rough because she works too hard, and has no butter to smear into them at the end of the day. She

159

has no butter, has never had, and will not—till her calf grows up and gives fresh milk.

Ta'Angzoum moves fast to keep her balance, stepping only on the second, fourth and fifth rungs of the ladder, knowing which will support her weight and which will not. With a deft kick at each step, she avoids tripping over the spotted blue robe wrapped clumsily around her. Is she attractive, Ta'Angzoum? Dressed in her red rayon shirt for village festivals she can be presentable, but not right now, not with soot on her face and black beads of sweat quivering in beads on her nose. Her matted hair, braided days ago, is as dull as the coat of her calf. Her eyes flit quickly over the veranda as she reaches the top of the ladder. Her movements are necessarily mannish. She jumps up from the last rung to the veranda. She stoops. She gently shoves the calf off her shoulder.

Ta'Angzoum stops awhile to catch her breath, glancing over the white walls and dark windows of the village huts. Her eyes pause at any hint of movement within the windows. Sometimes she thinks she sees him, the one she last saw four days ago flirting with the girls by the river: her husband. Sometimes she knows it is just her imagination. 'He's off,' Lobsang Norbu's wife had said this morning in the fields, 'chasing young girls by the river.' Ta'Angzoum raises a sleeve to her face and wipes off the sweat. Then she watches the calf settle down in the sunshine, and she feels its comfort in her bones.

She checks to make sure there's enough grass on the veranda to last the calf all day. Then, with another sweeping glance across the village huts, Ta'Angzoum enters the pitch blackness of the upstairs room. In its shadows she sees the silhouette of the kettle against the orange embers of the stove. Her mother is heard wheezing in a corner. Ta'Angzoum scoops up the kettle and pours butter tea into the dim curves of her mother's tea cup. Crouching on to the burlap rug she blows into the fire, adding to it a handful of goat pellets for fuel. She blows again and again. The flames light up her shiny eyes, and sweat springs up on her nose. Soot and ash fly into the air and fall on her hair, her face and hands. She tastes thick smoke in her mouth as she places the buckwheat gruel on the stove.

Ta'Angzoum hopes her mother is well enough to take Pasang Thondup's cows to the pastures today. There are other matters she herself must attend to. Last night her brother said he would help renegotiate her wages with the man whose fields she weeds each morning. A few handfuls of buckwheat seeds aren't enough for all that work, that's what her brother had said. Ta'Angzoum hopes he wasn't too drunk when he said this; she hopes he'll remember his offer of help today.

She serves her mother hot buckwheat gruel, then fills her own bowl, lifting it to blow on it before she sips. She studies her mother's dark outlines, listens for her asthma, and murmurs, 'You're breathing easier today.'

Her mother moans, but it is wheezing Ta'Angzoum listens for. The wheezing debilitates her, keeps her from the pastures. Ta'Angzoum ventures, 'I was thinking of speaking to Karma today about raising my wages.' But her mother doesn't respond, and Ta'Angzoum knows, she understands, for this is the way they communicate, that she will have to mind Pasang Thondup's cows so that her mother can spend the day in the sun beside the calf, chanting her endless prayers and supplications.

When the gruel is finished Ta'Angzoum carries the dirty bowls out to the sun-soaked veranda and pours the leftover drops into a plastic jerry can beside the calf. She squints in the light, and reaches into the folds of her robe to add a handful of barley to the calf's jerry can. This is how she measures away every last grain she earns. She will receive a few measures of wheat tonight in return for taking Pasang Thondup's cows to the pastures. There will be wheat bread for her mother tonight. In the evening she'll go to her brother, hoping that he will repeat his offer of help. This, she thinks, is who she is. This is who she is. A woman who is always hoping. Her eyes dart about, searching for her husband in the windows of village huts despite the fact that she hates him, hates the claim he's made on her calf in his bid to separate. Months she has been waiting for village elders to settle their case and to declare the calf rightfully hers. Months she has waited for justice. She has pleaded before the village's most important men about her private hurts. 'He climbs over village rooftops in search of younger girls.' She has cried in front of everyone, even strangers. She asked for justice from the district chairman last month when he came riding a horse.

A light wind is shifting past the veranda now, stirring against her cheeks, and she gives herself over to its cool, soft, tickling flow.

Infrastructure: roads, trails and bridges. To be surveyed, cost-estimated, constructed, repaired and rehabilitated. Electricity: micro-hydros, mini-hydels. GI pipes, sacks of cement carried up by mules. Irrigation canals. River training along unstable embankments, rows of stacked gabion boxes. A second airport to increase trade and tourism. If not, a ropeway: how useful for exporting local vegetables and fruit—cabbages, plums, apples. How useful for setting up a transportation industry managed by a local contractor—which one?

The district chairman sits at his desk trying to compose his speech for the annual District Development Committee meeting coming up next week.

Infrastructure. His bifocals sit heavy on his nose. The page in front of him is blank. He must write a speech. His mind hums with ideas: roads, electricity, an airport or maybe two helipads.

He hunches over his desk and writes in a neat, sloping script: *We are the poor people of a poor, developing country.* He sits back and examines the sentence. There is theatricality to his actions. He is not alone in the room. Across his desk, in the shadows of his windowless office, are three lumpy sofas, all occupied. The first by an old Magar whose son was just jailed in a forest fire case. The old man is carrying a bundle of fresh cabbage, and his eyes, paled by cataracts, waver and blink in hesitation. Next to him is the chairman's young, twitching nephew here to see about his botched examinations. Will uncle talk to the district education officer? That's what he's here to say; it shows all over his sickly face, in the way he shifts in his chair, trying to catch the chairman's eyes but looking away when he does. To the nephew's side is the petty contractor Lal Bahadur, sitting with his hands folded and his chubby legs spread.

Without looking up from his speech, the chairman says, 'Bringing vegetables doesn't make a difference.' His flat, unconcerned tone produces the desired effect. The old Magar rustles to attention, and the petty contractor guffaws. The chairman peers over the rims of his bifocals. The old Magar is clutching his vegetables. His face is pulled back, and the thin fibers of his tunic are stretched taut. The chairman says, in the same blasé tone, 'Cabbages won't get your son out of jail.'

The petty contractor guffaws again, and the nephew smirks. The old Magar stands up and joins his palms in plea. 'He was asleep.' His voice comes out husky and hollow. 'He didn't mean to set the fire.'

The chairman raises an eyebrow. 'And so the cabbages prove this?' Delicately, he tucks the sheet on which he has just composed his first sentence. He adds, 'Or are they meant to give me the strength to walk over to the judge's office and ask him to release your son?'

The old Magar blinks uncertainly. 'A man as strong as you,' he mumbles, 'what would one dry cabbage do...' Meekly, he adds, 'And a chairman wouldn't have to go to a judge.'

At this the contractor Lal Bahadur guffaws a third time, and the nephew begins to shake his legs. Realizing he's being played with, perhaps, the old Magar smiles cautiously. 'For the district chairman...' He holds up the cabbage.

The chairman waves his hands in a dismissing gesture. 'Give it to your son in jail.' He feels a sudden urge to compose another sentence. We are the poor people of a poor, developing country...

'Give it to your son,' Lal Bahadur repeats in that richly intoned voice of contractors, a melodic, suggestive voice that pleases the chairman. The contractor unfolds his arms, puts his hands in the pockets of his jacket and spreads his plump legs wider. To the old Magar, he says confidently, 'Old man, don't worry about your son. Tell him to wash the clothes of the police, polish their shoes, cook their food, they'll love him. In jail, he won't have to work all day chopping wood.'

Darting a glance at the chairman, the nephew shrilly adds, 'Yeah.'

The old Magar smiles ruefully. 'His wife, his children.' He fixes his pale, cataracted eyes on the chairman. 'My grandchildren, growing up without a father. My son's mother can't stop crying.'

Brusque now, the chairman says, 'Go, old man.' Why doesn't the old Magar just go straight to his house past the high school, meet his dear dimpled wife and drop off the cabbage? That's what everyone else does. The chairman says, 'Give those vegetables to your son and come back in a week, I'll see what can be done. But you understand,' he says sternly, 'there's almost nothing that can be done.'

The old Magar shuffles out.

'If only they came with reasonable requests,' the chairman says in a genial, confiding tone to the contractor. Then he turns to his nephew. 'Your mother told me about your matter. I'll do what I can.'

His nephew doesn't understand this as a dismissal, and he reaches up to feel the pimples on his face. Haltingly, he asks, 'It's been done, then?'

'Not yet.' The chairman turns down to squint at the nearly empty page on his desk. 'These things take time, you know.'

The nephew shifts in his seat.

The chairman frowns. 'There's nothing else, then? Just that little matter?'

His nephew takes leave.

Which leaves only the petty contractor. The chairman takes off his bifocals and rubs his eyes. 'Tea?' He rings the bell under his desk and a peon shows up at the door. He orders two cups. 'This speech,' he says then. 'Not a minute to write it...' He looks down at the near-blank sheet of paper.

Lal Bahadur asks, 'Is there much construction planned for this year?'

Which reminds the chairman about infrastructure. Roads, trails, bridges, electricity, airports, ropeways: how useful for awarding contracts. He says, 'One or two.'

'The Baglung road?' The contractor's legs come together and cross.

'Not this year,' the chairman says. The contract for the Baglung road—if funds for that project get approved—will go to his brother-in-law, who will funnel back a percentage to his dear dimpled wife. He says, 'There are a few other big projects, like that road to the high school. And the bridge to Syaule Bajaar.'

'That's the metal bridge?'

'The metal bridge.' The chairman has a flash of inspiration. 'Just a moment, Lal Bahadurji.' He puts on his bifocals and rereads the first line of his speech: *We are the poor people of a poor, developing country.* We are the poor people of a poor, developing country? No. He crosses out *country* and replaces it with *nation.*

Honourable Member of Parliament, Chief District Officer Sah'b, Acting Local Development Officer Sah'b, District Judge,

District Superintendent of Police Sah'b, Office Chiefs and Acting Office Chiefs from the Offices of Education, Housing and Physical Planning, Public Health, Forestry, Drinking Water, and Non-Government Organization Chiefs, Village Development Committee Chairmen and Vice-Chairmen, Prominent Politicians, Social Servants, and Well-Wishing Brothers and Sisters,

We are the poor people of a poor, developing nation.

(Say something about our historic deprivation etc., especially being a remote district. <u>Live in the shadows of death rather than the shadows of the Himalayas.</u>) Must spend our resources on the poorest of the poor.

OUR PARTY. With new decentralization laws allowing the District semi-autonomous decision-making powers about its own development, this will finally become possible. For this I would like to thank OUR PARTY. When I met with HONOURABLE PARTY CHIEF last month at PARTY MEETING in Kathmandu, I thanked him in person on the podium. (Emphasize: I was one of the ten District Development Committee Chairmen seated at podium.)

It is with pride, therefore, that I preside over this meeting in order to plan our district's development activities for the upcoming fiscal year.

INFRASTRUCTURE: As you know, life in our remote district is very, very hard, without even the most basic infrastructure. Where are the roads that will facilitate our transportation, the airports that will bring in more tourists, the river training that will stabilize our embankments, the irrigation canals that will water our fields? Where is the electricity with which our children may read at night? Particularly in remote districts such as ours, many villages lack even the most basic infrastructure, like trails leading to pastures. How many hectares of arable land have we lost due to erosion of river embankments? And how many of our brothers and sisters have we lost to road accidents stemming from dangerous paths? Many of our villages don't even have a proper house to keep our government offices in.

(Talk about the infrastructure built since I've been in office. FRUITS OF DEVELOPMENT. GOD-GIVEN RIGHTS. IN THIS PROUD NATION.) FOR WHAT CAN WE DO WITHOUT ROADS AND BRIDGES, WITHOUT ELECTRICITY? In this regard, I am very happy with the construction work undertaken by the various government and non-government offices active in our district. The projects to be undertaken by the District in the upcoming fiscal year are aimed at supporting the efforts of these offices.

Among others, these works include:

1. Construction of a two-kilometre road from the district airport to the river, ending at the high school;

2. Feasibility survey and cost-estimation for an airport in Chele village, which I visited only last month;

3. Feasibility survey and cost-estimation for a road to the city road head;

4. Massive rehabilitation of the metal bridge to Syaule Bajaar;

5. Feasibility survey and cost-estimation for a hydropower plant in the district headquarters;

6. River training along the south end of the airport.

(Make the Vice-Chairman read out the whole list.) EMPHASIZE POINT ABOUT OPEN COMPETITION BETWEEN

CONTRACTORS. MENTION NATIONAL DEVELOPMENT TRENDS, GLOBAL TRENDS, etc. EVERYONE NEEDS DEVELOPMENT.

ALL-PARTY CONFERENCE: In addition, I would like to inform everyone that I will do my utmost in Kathmandu when I attend next month's All-Party Conference to stress the importance of the Baglung road for our district's economy.

<u>Mention opposition's efforts to undermine government, but end in conciliatory tone.</u>

Ta'Angzoum, wandering among the cows in pastures far away from the district centre, gave the chairman the line: we are the poor people of a poor, developing country. She stands now amid a field of anemones, staring at their quivering white petals and spiky green leaves. She plucks one flower and chews absently on its stalk. Yes, she is the one who pleaded, when the chairman came riding a horse last month. All she wanted was for him to declare the calf legally hers. She had meant to make her appeal more pressing by crying out, 'We are the poor people of a poor, developing country.' But he just rode away, leaving her to the crowds of villagers, clucking, 'This isn't the time, girl, this isn't the time to tell everyone about your private quarrels.'

But that was the time.

Ta'Angzoum wanders now in the pastures, thinking of her calf. She thinks of her mother. She thinks of herself. She is a generous woman. So much—fresh milk, small comforts, her mother's health, her life, her whole identity—depends on letting those in power have their due.

The anemone stalk tastes pleasantly astringent in her mouth.

The Newly Appointed Chemistry Professor

~

On the way to the campus, the newly appointed chemistry professor took shelter behind men. She followed them as they walked through crowds, slipped behind them as they shoved past students, took the space they made for her with the wide berth of their shoulders. She swerved when they swerved, stopped when—seeing a friend across the street—they stopped. She was thankful for the protection they gave. The campus was almost entirely male, full of men—boys, students—with eyes that darted, lips that smirked. In class, the backbenchers hissed and jeered at her soft voice, her shifting movements, as though she had given them an invitation to abuse: she knew the power the fear the pinch of grasping hands. Fear was imprinted in her flesh. Measure, measure. She tried to keep her fears in check. A woman once raped is not exposed to all. She tried to breathe in calmly as she walked through the campus sheltering from men by hiding behind other men.

The Eldest Son Thinks of Home

~

At Chicago's Lincoln Zoo the tamarind monkeys with saffron tails and droopy white whiskers frisked about in a cage with a background of painted blue skies. The sky in the snow leopard's cage was cloudy. I saw a ten-year-old screaming at his mother; I looked for some pure emotion and tried not to stare at lovers embracing. That was how I spent my day today. At night, in the drugstore, a sign announced it was National Ice Cream Month. A magazine I read recently said that America's is the most overweight society of the planet. Father, I'll send you half my first month's salary as soon as I find work. It is unbearably hot here. The air sticks to the skin in humidity. I pray all is well in the village. The tile flooring of my rented room reminds me of the corner shop where I used to buy you loose sticks of Yak cigarettes.

Tilled Earth

~

Antipodes: places opposite each other. Not long ago she used to study in a square patch of sun in a classroom while white motes of dust sparkled above and bluebottles zoomed by her ear. Eucalyptus trees spiced the air. Now, in Seattle's misty shadows, she reads, *'Values' are concepts about right and wrong, and about desirable and undesirable, normal and abnormal, proper and improper.* She is too old to believe America's myths. She reads: *Generally, Americans have very little information about other countries and their people.* She lives in a tidy room with bare cream walls with a view on to a rain-drenched alley off Olive Street.

Bolt-hole: a hole in the ground into which a pursued animal flees. She fingers the windowpane and its sleek, glassy surface, as simple as her life in the past few months. Cool, cold. Slip. *Clean break.* Her fingers trace a trail through the fine brown dust. *Keep to the right*, it says in the book she bought in Kathmandu. She knows better than to believe what it says, but still, in the early mornings, she leafs through it. *Line up*, it says, *and wait your turn, first-come, first-served. Don't block the traffic, don't block the view. Ask permission before you smoke.* The glass is crossed with clean, curved finger marks.

She wakes up one night and—seeing the crisp creamy edges of the ceiling—can't remember where she is. She thinks she hears a human sigh in-between sirens echoing in the dark. The people she shares the house with intimidate her. They talk too fast in unintelligible twangs. She is unsure about the people she sees in the streets. Her classmates at the community college are so animated. She doesn't move the way they do. She watches them.

Caldera: a large volcanic depression. She knows she has to make friends with Americans, and joins a group of her classmates at Denny's after American history. She smiles through their banter and gets unsettled by questions she doesn't know how to ask. They are talking about cartoons they watched growing up. Her thoughts stray to memories of the plump flesh of aubergine, of burned fenugreek and spinach. Bitter gourd is her favourite dish, deep fried with slices of okra. Her lover used to say, 'In the heat it gives you energy.' She finds that she whispers to herself in Nepali at bus stops, at doorways, in the shower, in bed in the middle of the night.

Dell: a wooded hollow or valley.

'Yeah, yeah.' 'No way.' 'Sure thing.' 'See you.' 'Hey there.' 'Later.' 'Get out of here.' Dot your i's and cross your t's. Words seem to mock her when she tries to speak about her life in Nepal to one of her housemates, Mariana, originally Russian, and now American, who seems to be irritated when she has to stop to listen. If she were Indian she could explain herself better. Everyone here knows India. She reads: *Americans see themselves as separate human beings who are responsible for their own decisions, and assume everyone else in the world is too.*

There is a woman in the community college, Jenny, an older married classmate who slows down to listen to her more than the others do. To Jenny she says, one day, 'Everyone lives with their family there. We do not like to live alone.' But later she realizes she is wrong; she would have preferred solitude there, freedom from her family and society. She could have if she had broken all the rules, as some women do. But it is not possible to explain these complexities to Jenny. And so she repeats, 'We do not live alone.'

Errand of mercy: a journey to relieve suffering. A Baptist preacher and his wife who have volunteered to be her host family take her around and tell her about Seattle. They say it is the home of America's best coffee. In a shop she sees hand-painted mugs shaped like the copper measuring pot for grains back home. She buys one mug and decorates her empty shelf with it. One evening, after physics class, she goes to the apartment of another student and drinks microbrewery beer, which she finds bitter and doesn't like. At twenty-six she has never tasted beer before. After that outing, she can recognize the sweet smell of malt when she passes a brewery. She is not particularly isolated. The Baptist preachers drive her on weekends to local beaches, parks and rivers, and talk to her fondly about the Northwest. They point at the Cascades, the Olympics and Mt Rainier when the sky is clear. She asks them questions she knows they will like:

Tilled Earth

about their church and about their faith. She listens to the sounds around the words they respond with. The rain patters through her letters about America.

Feud: a plot of land held under the feudal system.

She talks to Jenny about the classes she used to take in Nepal: biology, zoology, forestry. She left college after two years. She feels that the American education system is better. She admits, 'I did not like to study there.' Jenny tells her about her family, originally from Akron, Ohio. She asks more about Nepal. They talk for an hour over coffee. Afterwards, she feels elated, having said something about her past that makes sense in her present.

On her forms she is a non-resident alien, and she is smiling in front of a blue drop cloth.

Her closest relative, a distant cousin, lives in Indiana, illegally. Can she afford to call him? She picks up the phone and dials and gets an answering machine. She hangs up.

She avoids Mariana and her other housemates and they seem to avoid her. She finds herself growing unnerved each time they pass her in the halls or the common living room. In her room, her days pass manageably. People talk too fast here. She herself moves slowly, formulating full sentences before she speaks. She wonders if she can afford to call her lover. She calls her cousin instead.

'Have you applied for a credit card? Apply for a credit card. On your campus, you'll see people at booths. Visa, MasterCard, American Express. You have opened a bank account, haven't you? Just go to Jack In The Box and say you're looking for a job.

Don't say you're not American. They won't ask, I promise they won't. If they do, say you're American. Do you have a social security card? First go and get that, then. You need to get a social security card for anything in this country. Wait—what's your address? I'll write to you instead, with a list of things you have to do at once.'

Graphicacy: ability to read a map or graph. One night she wakes up and recognizes the cream fields of the ceiling and bare walls, and feels dulled by the recognition.

Some days she feels a sharp, undirected longing for everything she sees, even asphalt damp with sleet, reflecting winter clouds. These longings come suddenly, and give way to the throb of nostalgia for the grey of early morning fog, the bone-chill of her childhood winters. Nostalgia soon passes into pain as she thinks about her lover. The rain in Seattle stirs desire in her guts, and the halogen glow of the night road makes her cry, suddenly, as she rides home on the bus.

Heartland: the most central part of a region. Hinterland: a fringe area. Heath. Hollow.

It has been months and she still hasn't learned how to talk to her classmates. Sometimes she remains too reserved, and sometimes she says things that are too intimate. Afterwards she avoids those to whom she has said too much. Jenny is the only one to whom she has explained why she left college early. 'He taught in the university. There is only one university in Nepal. He was my forestry professor.' Jenny seems not to judge her, but speaks harshly of her lover. American woman. 'A professor? That's really bad—but it's not your fault,' Jenny says.

How could she understand? There is so much else about the relationship that she can't tell Jenny about. He is fourteen years older, with the cut features of a Gurung man. Jenny asks about his caste. Caste. 'He was from another whole tribe.' She doesn't tell Jenny that he is going to visit her and the two of them will marry.

In Nepal her parents wouldn't let them.

So much is left unspoken.

When Americans encounter a person from another culture who is concerned with following tradition, they often say that this person is indecisive, unsure or weak.

Every now and then, she gets an email. My love, it says in the subject heading.

There is a Jack In The Box seven blocks from Olive Street. Its floor is covered with orange tiles, and its tables with dark wood veneer. Above every table there is a hanging lamp. A few people are waiting in front of the counter, where two teenage girls are taking orders. There are restrooms to one side, next to another door that says Employees Only. She chooses one of the lines in front of the counter.

What to do if the Immigration and Naturalization Service tries to question you:

1. Remain silent and do not answer any questions. Give them your name. But do not tell them when you were born, how

or when you entered the United States, or if you have any documents.

2. You are allowed by law to call your family or a lawyer. Memorize the phone numbers of your family members.

3. Do not sign anything without talking to a lawyer.

The Baptist preachers invite her to a Sunday service every week, in a church with high echoing walls. Lately she has begun to make excuses not to go. She wants to see them less; she doesn't like the way they make her feel like a foreigner. These days she finds herself 'taking care of business'. 'Running errands.' She gets her eyes checked, visits a dentist, applies for an identity card and a social security card. Her parents send her a letter saying that she is halfway through the year, and they hope she is safe, and eating regularly. The winter fogs are thick in Kathmandu. It is her lover's letters she waits for.

Idiolect: the form of language used by an individual person. Forty-one cents in change takes long to count, so she hands the checkout clerk a dollar. She should have bought an umbrella with a curved wooden handle—this one might be hard to hold. The clerk is always friendly to her. Today he says, 'There are some flower fields up north I could take you to.' She shakes her head no, politely. She must remember to buy a glove because it's so cold these wet winter days. He says, 'Give me a call, some time.' She notices that she's long stopped converting dollars into local currency, one to seventy. She's heard that the exchange rate has got worse since she left.

On the phone, her cousin agrees: 'Yeah, the dollar is strong these days.' His voice on the phone is soothing. She understands that he is trying to ease her move into a new life, and she says, 'Yes.' She tells him about the job she tried to get at Jack In The Box. It scared her to approach the manager, she confesses. She left before he came out of the kitchen.

He says, 'Try McDonald's. Try Burger King. Don't be afraid, that's the most important thing. Pretend you're American.'

Junction: an act or instance of joining. The man from the grocery store calls about the flower fields and she doesn't know how to say no. His name is Allen. She calls him back a day later and says she can't go. The man will not take her, she thinks, to where she wants to go. It is the right decision. That week, she receives a letter from Nepal. The handwriting belongs to her lover. She holds the envelope to her chest till she gets to her bedroom, where she tears it open. My love, it begins, my love.

Jurisdiction authority supervision power prerogative dominion say control ride influence province district territory compass range sphere of influence reach, she clutches. She feels numb when she puts down the letter. It is the distance that makes his words sound unnatural. Perhaps she has got unused to Nepali, to the way they used to talk. Perhaps she has started to think with American words.

The phrases Americans use express their respect for individualism: 'Do your own thing.' 'I did it my way.' 'You'll have to decide that for yourself.' 'You made your bed, now lie in it.' 'If you don't look out for yourself, no one else will.' 'Look out for number one.'

She puts the letter away.

She emails him: I am glad that you are coming to me.

She must get a job at once.

It is unlawful for the Immigration and Naturalization Service or Police to detain you or to check your documents just because of your foreign appearance.

'Excuse me, sir, I am wondering if you have any job openings.'

'Excuse me please, there is a sign on your window saying you have a job?'

She goes out to dinner with Jenny and Jenny's husband, Mike, an architect who is tall and has crooked ears and big hands and gentle, attentive manners. They ask her many things about Nepal. He talks about a trek he once took in Kashmir, India. It makes her feel understood that he has visited India. As the evening wears on, she begins to feel euphoric. 'My boyfriend, he is coming,' she tells them in an unguarded moment.

'For a visit?' Mike asks, and she hesitates.

'That's wonderful,' Jenny says in a neutral tone.

Afterwards, she wonders what kinds of friendships are formed here. There is so much she hasn't told Jenny—about her job, about the fact that she and her lover were planning to get married after he came. She feels like she is betraying Jenny with her silence.

The smell of meat doesn't bother her, or the heat in the Burger King kitchen. She likes the orderliness of her work, and enjoys the sensations that accompany it. The whirring of the fans hush out the hiss of the stove, the purr of potatoes deep-fried. She likes the hard feel of metal against her. She has many co-workers who come for four- or six-hour shifts. Mostly, she is with Denise, a girl who is still in high school, and Matt, who is older—maybe twenty. They feel like younger siblings to her. Matt talks constantly about whatever comes to mind. The fan in his car broke down and the latest Bruce Willis movie sucks. The best park in Seattle is Discovery. His family came from Hong Kong when he was nine, and his father died within a year. His stepfather is a cool guy.

She likes his prattle, and likes Denise's friendly banter, and can't get the sound of the fans out of her ears at night.

Two months till he arrives. She tries to imagine him stepping off the plane at Sea-Tac International Airport, and can't.

Know by name: be able to give the name of.
   Know by sight: recognize only the appearance of.
   Know how: know the way to do something.
   Sometimes she blurs her vision and walks for hours through a haze of colour and light, through fields of grey, blues that shine and shiver her blood as cool as the dew that covers the city. Ether, the shapes that blur by, shifting with each step. The air is moist in this yearlong monsoon of her life. Many of the plants she recognizes from home. Holly. Magnolia. Rhododendron. Rhododendron is Nepal's national flower, but she's never seen them close-up, the way she sees them in Seattle: these large, floppy, unscented red and pink flowers.
   Two months is a long time. One day, on impulse, she buys shorts and begins to run; she likes the unfamiliar feeling of her

body in motion. It is something she could never have done back home, where her legs were veiled. This is another woman running. This is a 'whole new you'. She has stopped writing to her lover, knowing that it won't be long now before she sees him in flesh.

Ley farming: alternate growing of crops and grass. Her lover calls, his voice is deep and gentle, and he says he's booked a flight. He repeats the details of his flight two times. 'It goes to Hong Kong, then Osaka.'

'I took the same flight,' she says both times.

'My family knows I'm going to stay in America.'

These words don't sound right in this room.

Macadam: a road made of layers of compacted broken rocks.

Notation: a set of symbols, a record. At the seashore with the Baptist preachers she thanks them for having introduced her to America. This, she has decided, is the last time she will accept any of their invitations. 'We certainly hope to have you over more often than we have,' they say brightly. She thanks them again and smiles and repeats how wonderful it has all been. The sky presses low against the ocean, and the fog rolls in, obscuring the line where sky ends and waves begin. She is facing west, towards Asia. Her heart begins to pound, and pound.

Every time she passes by the library she continues to search the American Heritage Dictionary for words that will help her speak about her new life. Oceanic. Patter: tiptoe, scurry, scuttle, skip, scamper. Quaquaversal: pointing in every direction. Ramble: amble, meander, wander, stroll, saunter, walk, range, rove, hike, trek. Redetermine. Redefine.

She calls her lover at midnight Kathmandu-time and hangs up before anyone answers. He calls her back midnight Seattle-time, and she is waiting by the phone. 'I'm not sure any more,' she says. 'What if it's a mistake?'

'It's not a mistake.'

'I don't know.'

'I can't cancel the ticket.'

'I don't know.'

She thinks about it, and thinks about it, before she formulates this story: there was a woman, she says to herself. She grew up in a very traditional society, where women were considered the property of men—either their father or their husband. Now this woman, one day, met a man who loved her, who she couldn't marry because…and here she falters…he was too old, let's say, and in any case you couldn't marry the person you loved; there was a system of arranged marriage, which is why the woman's family wanted her to marry a man she didn't love. She wouldn't do that. To make sure she could not meet her lover, her family confined her at home. But they confined her so long she began to fall in love with a larger dream of freedom. She didn't love her lover any more, and she didn't love her parents. She just wanted to escape. But one day, when she met her lover in secret, he said, 'Be my wife,' and she couldn't refuse because she could see attachment in his eyes. She told herself she loved him very much.

Her pay cheque comes in, just under two hundred dollars every two weeks. Her pay cheque comes every two weeks. Every day after work she runs, lifting her feet higher, stepping further. What she likes above all is feeling light between steps. She takes new paths each time and doesn't mind it when she loses her way.

Sanctuary. Scree: a slope covered with small, loose stones. Trammel: an impediment to free movement. Ulterior: existing in the background. Vacillate. Walled. Xenophobia.
   'It's just wrong, there's something wrong with it.'
   'There's no choice, I can't cancel it.'
   'There's something wrong with it, I don't want you to come any more.'
   'Is it final, then?'
   'There's nothing wrong with it.'
   'I don't know, it seems wrong, there's something wrong.'

Finding mercy in a phone that won't ring, an email that won't come, a letter that won't arrive.

There once was a woman. She listens to the other students discuss what classes they're taking next year, and what they're doing over the summer. She doesn't tell any of them that she won't be back next year. She feels ashamed, humiliated by the thought that people may intuit her plans. 'Illegal alien.' She listens to herself saying these words, and doesn't like their bitter inflections.

She learns to work the cash machine, and to talk to the customers, but she most enjoys the prattle between Matt and Denise in the kitchen, which she has learned how to join. 'I don't like the food at Dick's,' she says, hearing them talk about the diner across the street.

'Their food sucks,' Denise agrees, but Matt says that when you're drunk there's nothing better to stabilize your system.

At the end of the school year, Jenny and her husband invite her over for dinner. Mike is nice to her, but tends to explain more than he has to. 'Pesto is made up of basil and pine nuts.' Even Jenny's questions seem remote. 'Do you eat salad in Nepal?'

'When I was trekking in Kashmir we didn't eat anything that hadn't been cooked thoroughly.'

As she passes around the endives, the rolls and olive oil, she realizes that these are people who appear like a dream in her life, and are gone. She won't remember their faces a year from now.

'I understand you'll be spending the summer with some relatives in the Midwest?'

Yearlong: lasting a year. She has become incomprehensibly attached to the blank cream surface of her room. She tells Mariana that she will be leaving at the end of the month, and agrees when her housemates tell her to post notes on campus billboards, asking for a new roommate. 'Sure,' she replies. 'No problem.'

Americans place a premium on efficiency.

'I'm going to Indiana to live with my cousin. Even if you come to Seattle, I won't be here. I'm leaving in two weeks.'

'It's final, then?'

'It's final.'

The last time they talk, he says, 'I love you.'

In English, it sounds grotesque.

Becoming illegal she waits by a dark window, listening to the rain beat against the tar of the alley outside, aching because the bare cream walls that flicker with halogen shadows are so beautiful.

You and yours: you together with your family and property. On the phone with her father, she speaks the thirty-six consonants and twelve vowels of Nepali a little less quickly than she used to. She tells him that she is going to live with her cousin, and he shouldn't worry about her. She repeats this same message to her mother, three times. She doesn't tell them that she will be illegal, or that she may never finish her schooling or return home. She wouldn't know how to tell them such things; these are messages the Nepali language does not relay.

That's neither here nor there. In Nepali, the expression goes: 'Neither from here nor from there.'

Zero-sum: a situation in which whatever is gained by one side is lost by the other so that the net sum is always zero.

There was a woman who decided to rewrite her life story, she thinks. To rewrite her life story—and she does, but in a language that is completely foreign.

When she says goodbye to Denise, they exchange friendship bands and say, 'See you.' Matt gives her a hug and says good luck with things and take care.

Jenny says, 'Have a good summer and enjoy your time with your family.'

Her housemates just say goodbye.

There once was a woman.

There once was a woman who.

For hours before she takes the bus to the airport, she stands at the window of her room, looking on to the alley off Olive Street, wracked by longing for what she can't return to.

The warm vapours of tilled earth, her lover's breath.

The European Fling

~

Somehow, the dates worked out perfectly. Sharada was due to
attend a seminar in Aix-en-Provence in late December, on
'Women in/against War', so she emailed Matt, who had always
proposed that they have a fling in Europe. She told him she
could take two weeks off afterwards, before returning home.
Matt emailed back within twenty-four hours: he could fly in
from New York, and they could go from Paris to Berlin to
Rome. He offered to make all the bookings on the internet.
Sharada emailed back: 'It's a date.' They arranged to meet at the
Gare du Sud on 31 December. The two of them had slept
together one drunken night, years back at Boston University,
but they had never got around to pursing sex again, despite
their ongoing friendship. Their emails became coy as the end of
December approached. 'Maybe we'll even fall in love,' Matt
wrote—a bit jarringly, Sharada felt—in an email she received in
Aix-en-Provence. She had learned from him—and in college it
had always been she who learned, he who taught—that love was
a bourgeois construct designed to entrap women's labour. Matt
had signed off his email with hugs and kisses. On the train to
Paris from Aix-en-Provence Sharada scanned the dark, furrowed
fields of the French countryside with a tingle of anticipation.

By the time Matt sighted her through the crowds at the Gare du Sud, he was tired by the taxi ride, plane ride and Metro ride: all the moving he had been doing since leaving the East Village. He hugged Sharada, noticing how snugly she was encased in her plump down jacket. Her eyes steadied upon his, searching out—what? He remembered how a request had always lingered in them. He kissed her because he felt that was what she expected. Then the warmth and wetness of her lips piqued his desire, so he kissed her again.

She felt buoyed by the crush of unknown people, by the fact that she was here at all. Paris! A European fling! She took no note of Matt's tired look. Taking his hand, she pulled him to the sign for the Metro. He was still so retro-chic. His jeans were cut above his ankles, and his white socks were showing between them and his oversize black shoes. He was wearing a lime green shirt and a black wool jacket. Sharada felt—dowdy—in her down jacket, but in the sharp winter cold she was grateful for its warmth. Matt's golden-brown hair was still long, falling in loose, untidy tresses. She had never liked long hair on men. There were bluish shadows under his eyes, and his cheekbones had come into gaunt prominence. 'You look great,' she said.

'It's weird being abroad,' he said as they rode the Metro. 'It's been a long time. Six, maybe seven years back he had gone to Vancouver. Since then it had only been Boston, New Haven, Cape Cod, or his parents, back in Cummington. Most days he didn't even leave the East Village. He wasn't proud of this; but there was that truism about New York, that it was possible to live there yet be part of everything. You didn't have to travel abroad to see the world.

On the train Matt seemed far away. Sharada squeezed his hand to pull him out of his reveries. She told him about the Aix-en-Provence conference. One delegate, a Venezuelan essentialist feminist, had got into a days-long tiff with an Indian delegate, a Naxalite, accusing her of being devoid of the essence of womanhood, which emanated not from the principle of class struggle, but from innate mother-love. 'The Naxalite looked like she just wanted to bomb the place,' Sharada said. Matt smiled wanly at the anecdote.

They got off at the Ile St. Louis station, and outside, by the Seine, consulted a guidebook that Matt had brought. Their hotel, a narrow eight-storey structure, was not far off. Though Matt had done the bookings, it was Sharada who dealt with the woman at the front desk, trying out her semester's worth of college French: it had served her well in Aix-en-Provence, and it served her well now. Standing silently by their luggage, Matt felt like an ugly American. In school he had taken Spanish; and though there were plenty of opportunities to use Spanish at home, he left his bookstore so seldom that he hardly spoke a word of any language other than English now.

The woman led them to a room on the third floor, a cramped den with gold-and-velvet wallpaper, and a bed and bureau occupying almost all the space. The bathroom was dank. The houses outside the window were crooked. Sharada loved the Parisian feel of it. Matt liked how small the room was, how insulated: like his East Village studio. He gave Sharada the Chomsky that he had been reading on the plane: 'I don't know if you've read this one.' Sharada thanked him. She was looking at him with the usual request in her eyes. And because Matt

Tilled Earth

needed to feel comfortable, and felt more comfortable doing this than anything else right now, he fished a condom out of his suitcase, pulled Sharada to him, and they made love.

If only all of life could be so fun, Sharada thought.

As they dressed for dinner, Matt wondered what there was to eat. He had been vegan, off and on, for two years, and vegetarian from college on. From the hotel they headed to the Quartier Latin. It was ridiculous to be vegan or vegetarian in France, he knew. All the French restaurants they passed smelled so— meaty. They stopped in front of Chinese, Vietnamese and Italian restaurants. Scrutinizing their menus, Matt found his mouth watering despite himself. Dim sum. Duck. Pizza. Provolone platter. He settled, at last, on crêpes: 'I guess there's no way to avoid a bit of dairy when you're travelling.'

In the crêperie Sharada noticed that Matt's gaze was landing everywhere but on her. 'Are you okay?' she asked. It was so draughty she kept her down jacket on, which made it hard to sit on the stool. 'You okay?' she asked, adjusting herself into place. Matt shrugged in reply. He did not know why, but he felt unprepared for the attention she was giving him. He should not have flirted with her over email, he realized. He was not up for a fling. And she was so plump now. To deflect her attention off him, he asked about her work, which, as far as he had understood from her emails, entailed offering village women interest-free loans to open shops and businesses, while at the same time teaching them about their legal and political rights. All Sharada told him was that she was bored with the work. 'It's just a job, you know? But I've done it so long now, I've become a top gender expert,' she said. 'If I have to attend one more conference I'll go mad! But I don't know what else to do.'

'When the whole system is so fucked,' Matt said, 'individual intervention achieves so little.'

'Do you feel that about your own work?' Sharada asked.

'What?'

'Does it feel pointless running a bookshop when your country is acting so stupid?'

Just then the waiter brought them their crêpes, and Matt stared in shock at the cream sauce slathered on top.

Sharada persisted, 'Do you feel your individual actions are futile?'

But Matt was too busy lopping the cream off his crêpe. It was frustrating to be locked out of language, to be reduced to such dumbness that he couldn't even tell the waiter: I didn't realize it came with cream. He ate what he could of the mushroom crêpe without fearing that he'd clog up his sinuses.

He suggested, after dinner, that they visit a bookstore. He had a list of shops that dealt in first runs and out-of-print editions. Sharada thought this a fine idea, so they went in search of one of the bookstores on the list, and found it in an alley of the Pompidou Centre.

Browsing the narrow stacks, Matt felt more at ease. How many hours, over the past years, had he spent browsing the stacks of bookstores? It opened him up. Afterwards, he felt more communicative. 'I'm going through a rough patch,' he said as he and Sharada walked back to the Ile St. Louis. He placed a thin arm around her wide-set shoulders. 'I guess I'm bored too, with my work.' He didn't like how soft he sounded, but he went on. 'There we are, all set up for circulating revolutionary, counterculture texts, right? I mean, I called the store Revolution Books. But most days I just stock books, or place orders, or do the accounts. I love being my own boss—how else would I ever get any health benefits? But it's been five years. I feel like I'm stagnating.'

'What would you rather do?' Sharada asked.

'I don't know. Something in the real world. After 9/11, you know… And the war in Iraq. I feel I should be doing more.'

Sharada remembered how light, how free life in the US had been for her—perhaps because she had been a foreigner. And as a student, even the politics on campus—post-feminism, neo-Marxism—had had a fey, entertaining quality: words were spun, there, for their own pleasure. Had things really changed after 9/11, after Iraq, she asked Matt.

'No, I guess it's always been shit,' he said.

He sounded so forlorn, she squeezed tighter into him to comfort him.

They reached the hotel and went up to the room, and Sharada lay on the bed, warming to the idea of sex.

'Is it all right if we don't make love?' Matt asked.

'Of course,' she said, feeling rejected. 'Yes, of course.'

Nothing ever came of the emails about falling in love. Over the next few days, succumbing to bouts of moodiness, Matt said he just wasn't feeling up for sex. 'You could play with yourself,' he suggested. 'You're a gender specialist. You know—that's the best way to make sure you actually come.'

'Thanks, but I can do that back home.'

Sharada was disappointed about this, but she composed herself. She wondered whether it was because she was fat. No.

Matt would be too much of a feminist to care. Still, it hurt a bit. But they were good friends, and she did want to preserve the friendship. So what if she hadn't had sex for years now? Nepal was dry that way. Most men past their mid-twenties were married. And those who weren't were intimidated by western-educated women like her. They preferred meeker, more docile women.

To cheer herself up she suggested, two days in, that they go to the Champs Élysées.

Matt balked. 'It'll just be like the postcards of it,' he said. 'That's such a tourist thing to do: to seek out simulacra, to go and see the image of Paris so that you feel like you're in Paris.' He said, 'But you go, if you want.'

'No, you're right,' she said, feeling as she used to, when they were in college. He had a more refined, theoretically sound sensibility; she had so much to learn from him.

But then, the only thing he wanted to do was visit bookstores. Day after day, Sharada tagged along with him to bookstores, seven of them, some in such bland modern neighbourhoods as the 16th Arrondissement. On the way to and from these bookstores, she eyed the Eiffel Tower with some wistfulness. Should she not be taking in the Louvre, the Musée d'Orsay? Where was the Sorbonne? What about Versailles? Or course Matt was right about the matter of simulacra. And she did appreciate the small rewards of staying away from the tourist areas. At one café in a tucked-away alley in a neighbourhood so nondescript it could have been anywhere in the world, Sharada ordered herbal tea, and the server directed a rush of breathy syllables her way: *C'est tout?* And she realized that she had passed for a local. She responded 'way', for *oui*, imitating the Aix-en-Provence accent.

Matt was content enough roaming the bookstores on his list. After all, if he had been a tourist visiting New York, the last thing he'd want to do was take in the Empire State Building, or Times Square. He had never even gone to Ground Zero—he had not avoided it, but nothing ever took him to the Financial District and, as time went on, he preferred to note the loss of the Twin Towers by their absence, the view of sky where there had been buildings. That seemed a more appropriate response for an insider. Besides, you met real people only if you went outside the tourist areas. At one bookstore, he ran into an American woman who was perusing the same narrow English books section. She smiled at him and he smiled back, and Sharada smiled too, and they all introduced themselves. Isabel was from a small town in Maine. She was working illegally at a brasserie in order to learn French cooking. 'Drop by some time,' she said. 'The food's fantastic. And it's not expensive at all.'

Matt thought it might be interesting to meet someone local—an insider, albeit an American. To Sharada, who was following him everywhere in a way that was beginning to irritate him, he suggested, as they left the bookstore, 'Shall we have dinner with her?'

'Who?'

'Isabel.'

'Sure.'

'She seems nice.'

'Sure.'

The Café d'Afrique was off a side street in Montparnasse. At work, Isabel was dressed in layers of black, with an extreme yet effortless elegance that seemed very French. She joined them during her tea break, and was full of lively stories about her culinary adventures in France. She talked about andouillette, champagne, fois gras with blackberry jam, salmon, all kinds of cheeses... But for each fey story she told them about herself, Sharada responded with a grim tale from back home: internal displacement, caste strife, war, the exploitation of women. Matt had no choice but to pay attention to these more serious issues. Sharada realized she was derailing the evening, but couldn't help herself. Why, Sharada wondered, did Matt look with such interest at Isabel? Why didn't he look at her that way?

The evening ended with her and Matt getting into a debate on Hindu fundamentalism in India, as Isabel watched on, bored, bemused.

That, pretty much, was Paris. For most of the long train ride to Berlin they were silent, except on banalities: 'I'm going to the bathroom.' 'Do you want a sandwich?' Looking out at the patchy fields of the former East Germany, Matt wanted very badly to be alone. Not—he told himself—that he didn't like Sharada. She had a down-to-earth approach to life that in college he had always been intrigued by. She came from an authentic background. She did what the Marxist-feminist critic Gayatri Chakravorty Spivak called the 'wild practice': she may not know much theory, but the work she did was genuine. Empowering village women. While all he did was run a bookstore. He felt—guilty—around her. Useless. Privileged. American.

Sharada flipped through the Chomsky that Matt had brought her, but only for the sake of politeness. When she had first read Chomsky, years ago, at Matt's urging, she had felt afire with his vision; but now it seemed that he stated the obvious, or what should be obvious to anyone who knew anything about the world. She would have thought Matt would have progressed on to new thinkers by now.

At the Zoo station, they were met by Matt's friend Steve, a conceptual artist from New York who had moved to Berlin a year ago. Steve was older, in his forties. Matt had told her, in a serious, awed tone, that Steve had exhibited at a leading gallery, Mary Boone: 'He's got a real head on him,' he had said. But to Sharada's relief, Steve had no arty airs. 'Welcome to Germany. Now remember: don't mention the war,' he joked, greeting them. He reminded Sharada of the less politically charged Americans she had met as a student in Boston. She immediately liked him.

After they settled into Steve's Karl Marxstrasse apartment—which had no heat, because Steve could not figure out how to light the wood-fire furnace—Matt said he wanted to take in a bookstore. Sharada sighed, but Steve said there was a small English bookstore on Rosa Luxemburgstrasse. So they went there, and browsed at length.

Almost since arriving in Berlin, Matt had found himself unnerved by the weight of history. The television tower at Alexanderplatz loomed nearby. The broad avenues were empty, and the buildings felt desolate, unattractive. The people in the bookstore were all white, and some looked poor, in a way that jarred. Night had fallen by the time he finished browsing. They headed back to Steve's apartment, and put together sandwiches. The apartment was absolutely freezing.

Sharada slept badly on the sofa, and woke up congested. She had worn her down jacket to bed, but all night her body had felt as cold as ice. In the bathroom she turned on the faucet but decided against washing her face. She returned to the living room to find Matt shivering on the sofa. 'Let's split,' he groaned.

They moved to a cheap pension off Kurfürstendamm, in a street full of brand-name shops.

Steve had a day off and offered to show them around. Sharada was glad for this. Matt, too, was glad to have him around. Maybe it was the cold: he just couldn't warm up to Berlin. It seemed to him that people here were—tense. Anxious.

As they walked around Ku'damm they both talked to Steve. 'It infuriated me, being in America,' Steve said. He sounded puzzled, though pleased, to be in Berlin. 'I was always so— fucked up. And so alone in being fucked up.' He laughed. 'Here I feel like everyone's fucked up. Like it's okay, or actually, it's the thing to do, to be fucked up. It's assumed you're totally fucked up.' He stopped and pointed at the Kaiser Wilhelm church. 'The Brits bombed it. Isn't it nice? The way it's just there, like an exposed wound.

'I could take you to Checkpoint Charlie,' he offered. 'Although there's nothing to see there. Or we could take in the Brandenburg date. Or the Victory Column—you know, that angel in Wenders's films. We could visit the library his angels meet in.'

Matt liked the idea, but at the U Bahn station he saw a scowling teenager with a shaved head. 'Let's go to some bookstores,' he said.

'No more bookstores,' Steve said, earning Sharada's gratitude.

They took the U Bahn to a café in Kreuzburg run by an American, someone Steve knew, a man named Gene, with greasy hair and a long rat-tail winding down his back. Matt asked Gene whether they were true, the reports that one read, now and then, about the rise of neo-Nazism.

'Oh, yes, yes, yes,' Gene said, emphatic. 'Depends on the area of course. I try not to walk around alone. I mean, I could pass for a German, right? Blond hair, blue eyes? But it just takes a few boys keeping track of you. These boys hate everyone, though of course if you're Turkish or something,' he glanced at Sharada, 'you're more of a target.'

'Even as an American you feel targeted?' Sharada asked, surprised.

'I have two friends—white Anglo-Saxon Americans—who were beaten up a few years ago. Well, one was just a mugging.' He said, 'Though muggers do target foreigners more. So it's not just a neo-Nazi thing. It's just a fact of life, I suppose.'

'What does it mean,' Matt asked, 'when you see boys with shaved heads?'

'Oh, that doesn't mean a thing,' Gene laughed. 'Not all neo-Nazis have shaved heads. It's far more complicated than that.'

Sharada was unnerved enough by this conversation to not mind spending the rest of the day walking from one Kreuzburg gallery to another, where Steve passed wry comments on the art on display: 'More angst. Angst redux. Angst denied.' They took the U Bahn back after dinner. Back on Ku'damm, Steve pointed out anything that might interest them, like an old, rusty Trabant parked beside a shiny black Mercedes and a polka-dotted Volkswagen: 'Like a postcard, isn't it?'

The next day, Steve left for Cologne to take in an art fair. Sharada suggested that Matt and she go and look at the Stasi headquarters on this, their last day in Berlin. But Matt said he wanted to spend the day in Kreuzburg, reading. When he said so, Sharada grew resentful. Matt had put aside Chomsky to read about Nazi atrocities, and his mood was very bleak. Of course it was a difficult thing to overlook: the Final Solution. But the war was long over. Matt was going overboard, Sharada felt.

'Have you noticed,' he asked as they left the pension, 'that people are always looking at us? They look so tense. It's like they're checking for foreigners.'

'It's the cold,' she snapped. 'It's just the cold. It makes people look unhappy.'

'Wannssee is on one of the U Bahn lines,' he said.

She said, 'So is a concentration camp. Sachsenhausen. Shall we go there?'

'This is all so freaky. I don't think I could deal with it.'

Sharada decided to set off on her own. Not to the concentration camp. She wanted to have a bit of fun. She took the U Bahn to the museums—or she tried to. Infected by Matt's paranoia, she was worried that she looked like a foreigner, so she didn't consult any maps. In one train, a thin East Asian man stood across from her, giving her a vacant, drugged-out stare. A pasty white man in the next aisle kept glancing menacingly at the East Asian man. Growing jittery, Sharada missed her stop, and then—making a wrong connection—she got lost. Finally she just took a connection to Kreuzburg.

She found Matt in Gene's café, and she flopped down on the chair next to him, feeling defeated.

They spent the entire afternoon reading in the café. Sharada put aside the Chomsky and read *Bridget Jones's Diary*, enjoying its utter frivolity. Matt was deep into some David Grossman essays on Israel and Palestine. He was more communicative that evening. 'I've never been pro-Zionist,' he said over his dinner of asparagus sandwich. She had ordered a plate of falafel. 'I've got so many Jewish friends in New York,' he said. 'Sometimes I wish I were Jewish. I've always liked their sense of being part of a diaspora: a scattered, wandering mass. Even they're not into Zionism. But I don't know any more. I can understand people wanting to have a homeland. Some place you really belong. It would be so important to you if you didn't have one,' he said. 'Like the Palestinians, the Kurds. The East Timorese.' He said, 'You know, I just don't feel at home in America.'

'The United States.'

'The United States. I don't even feel like I belong in New York.'

'Well, not *feeling* at home is a different matter,' Sharada said. 'But you're from the US and, whether or not you like it, that's a homeland that many would die for. You live in New York, for god's sake. Do you know how amazing that is?'

Matt took this in. 'Yes, of course.' He looked at her, and realized that he had been insensitive. Sharada lived, after all, in a Third World country. Women there were denied the most basic rights. Life there could not be easy. Her emails over the past few years had been filled with despair. Matt watched her forking a piece of falafel, and felt a twang of—something. Guilt.

Suddenly he had a quite lyrical impulse. 'Hey, we should get married.' He reached over and held her hand. 'We could marry, just to rescue you, get you out of Nepal,' he said. 'And to spite the Republicans. You don't want any more aliens? Well, here's another one!'

Sharada went cold. 'I don't really need to be rescued,' she said, withdrawing her hand from his.

On the train ride to Rome they quarrelled. Matt had made an off-the-cuff remark on Nawaz Sharif's demise as the end of democratic politics in Pakistan, and Sharada couldn't help but pounce, a bit shrilly, 'You like Nawaz Sharif?'

It wasn't as if he'd endorsed Hitler, Matt thought. 'At least he was better than Musharraf,' he said. 'At least he wasn't the army.'

'Don't tell me: you like Benazir Bhutto too.'

'Well, yeah.'

'Typical!' Sharada sputtered. 'Do you know that she made the laws for women more conservative than they used to be? But no. Americans think: oh, she's got a Harvard education, she's one of us.'

'That's not fair,' Matt cried.

'She sells you Americans all this crap about freedom,' Sharada continued, 'and you all are so ignorant, so simple, you buy it wholesale!'

'Oh, you can't be apologizing for Musharraf!'

'I'm not,' Sharada said, realizing that she was.

'Yes you are.'

'No I'm not.'

They both fumed a long while, as the German countryside passed by outside the train window, in the dark.

Tilled Earth

'In Rome,' Matt finally said, 'I think I need some space.'

'Space!' Sharada said. 'I need that too.'

The train pulled into Stazione Termini at ten in the morning, and they chose a nearby pension. The room had a view on to a dark cobbled road. The double bed made them both grimace, but this was the only room free in the pension, and sharing a room was cheaper than taking separate rooms.

Matt left immediately to find a café. Sharada consulted a map. The pension was only a few blocks from the Jewish quarters and Trastevere. She was determined to see some tourist sites at last.

Matt went into the Café Naoma because it looked dark and quiet, and he liked the graffiti on its door. Its interior was dimly lit, with tables so close you could hear everyone's conversations. He chose a table at the back, away from the windows. A man at the next table was working on a desktop. Matt leaned over, to peek at the screen. Yes. The man was on the internet. Beyond, along a line of tables, were several more computers, all unoccupied...

Sharada headed east along an irregular path that led past large stone houses. Were these ordinary houses, or expensive mansions? She could not tell. It was good to get away from Matt's incessant gloom. She had forgotten: he had always been depressive. In college he had always gone on about one massive problem or another... And of course the world was full of problems. Nepal certainly was. Everywhere you looked, there was a problem. This was supposed to be a holiday from all that.

The sun was out, casting the city streets into sharp relief. People here looked interested in life, energetic. Sharada felt cheered. At a crossroads she took a street leading north. The houses along this street had shuttered windows and rough granite walls. She had forgotten to bring the map; but if she remembered correctly, she would soon be reaching Trastevere.

At the Café Naoma, Matt was hunched over a desktop, on the internet. By now he had checked his mail, by habit first clearing out the spam and starring the messages that needed responding to. He was now going through these one by one. Isabel had written from Paris, and Steve from Cologne. He wrote back to both, flirting with Isabel and thanking Steve. Other friends had written as well. Derek, his assistant at Revolution Books, assured him that all was well. His friend Rafael's father in Santa Monica had fallen ill, and Rafael had gone to visit. Leah was in the Bahamas for the new year. His friend Judy, suffering a premature midlife crisis at thirty-five, was quitting Human Rights Watch to join Earth First. She had written: *most of the problems that humanss have we have created ourselves. we're shitheads, so we deserve to die in misery. but animals and the natural world don't deserve this. fuck, how's it going there? enjoying the old world?*

He read these emails again and again, feeling as though he were regaining his balance.

Sharada stepped through a stone archway, expecting to reach Trastevere, but instead found herself in a small, crowded courtyard lined by shops. Left or right? She went to a shop by the archway. 'Excuse me?'

The woman at the counter turned to her with a string of Italian words.

'Not Italian,' Sharada said, then ventured, 'Trastevere?'

From behind her, someone said, 'I am going just there. I will show you the way.'

She turned, and saw a young man of twenty, twenty-one. He looked Asian. He had long, jet-black hair, coppery skin and high cheekbones. From his knapsack she could tell he was a tourist. 'Thanks,' she said.

He bought a packet of cigarettes from the shop, then turned to Sharada. 'Come.'

It turned out the man was Tibetan. 'You are Nepali?' he said. 'Beautiful country. Many Tibetans are there.'

'Yes. Have you been?'

'Some day.'

'Well, I'd love to go to Tibet some day.'

He laughed. 'Me too.'

His name was Gyatso Tenzing. He was born and raised in Switzerland, near Bern. He spoke an oddly formal, textbook English: his first language was German, Swiss German. He was training to be a pharmacist, he said. Right now he was passing by Rome on the way to Naples, where he had friends. He said, 'If you are free we can go to the Coliseum also.' Then he took her through another archway, and they arrived at the wide plaza of Trastevere.

At the Cafe Naoma, Matt emailed Judy back. Travelling like a tourist had been a mistake, he wrote. 'You waste so much time, and you don't really learn anything you couldn't learn from reading a book. Earth Watch, wow,' he wrote. 'What will you be doing? Strapping yourself to trees?'

This kind of travelling Matt was happy to do. The following morning, he returned to the Café Naoma and surfed the web for hours. It got him back in touch with his world. He read the news and blog sites—Alternet, Huffington Post, Conscious Choice, *The Nation*—and felt back in known territory. When you travelled through texts, you could plumb the depths. He found an article about the growing trend of vegetarianism in France, and he read it. He read about the rise and fall of neo-Nazism in Germany. He read about the latest scandals in the Italian parliament. On a lark he also checked out job listings on several websites. Revolution Books. The problem was, no matter how bored he was with his work, he didn't really want to change too much. The bookstore was up and running, after years of struggle. It made him feel part of the counterculture. He had met most of his current friends in its aisles. And he liked his East Village routines. For someone from Cummington, New York had been so hard to break into: he finally felt like an insider, now, and didn't want to risk losing that. How could he possibly do anything more—meaningful, more important—while retaining his place?

The computer pinged as he surfed job listings. A friend, Keera, had emailed. He had met Keera in the Trotskyist section of the bookstore, and had immediately been drawn by her haunted, waif-like air. She was homeless at the time; he had let her share his flat for two weeks; they had slept together and remained friends afterwards. She wrote, in her email, that she was going to join a group of activists—Trotskyites—who travelled from state to state, protesting a variety of government policies. This wasn't a job per se, she wrote, but they did support themselves from the funds they raised. 'You should join us,' she had written. 'We're going to Idaho next month to lobby for pro-choice legislation.'

Matt stared out of the window of the Café Naoma. He, too, wanted a change. His life was so sheltered, so—safe. Or, discounting another terrorist attack on New York, it was safe. He had been seeking something different. Something—bigger. A real engagement with the wider world. Some wild practice, instead of just theory. Was that not why he had leaped at the chance to meet Sharada again? Was that not why he had come for this ill-conceived trip?

He sighed. From where he was sitting in the café, all he could see was a blank marble wall.

Gyatso had very nice lips: full, shapely and chocolate-brown. Sharada had never much liked long hair on men, but maybe because of his height it looked good on him. They met for a leisurely lunch near the Spanish Steps, and—like yesterday—instantly warmed to each other.

He told her about a trip he was planning to India. 'I want to go to Dharamsala of course. The centre of our government in exile. I want to get the blessings of the Dalai Lama,' he said. 'But I also want to go to other parts of India, and get to know the country, Bombay, Goa…'

'Trivandrum.'

'Pondicherry.'

'Khajuraho.'

'Khajuraho.'

After a lunch of fresh salad, pasta, fish and gelato, they headed to the Pantheon. It was easy to be in Gyatso's company: there was no discussion of politics between them, no occasion for pondering all that was wrong with the world. Of course, if she asked him about being Tibetan, there would be a lot to talk about. She did not ask him about it. And she did not talk about her own work. She felt light at last; she felt free. And she felt attractive, too. Gyatso was five, or maybe seven, years younger than she. Yet he was unmistakeably flirting with her. Was she so shallow? A leading gender specialist, she—. As they reached the Pantheon, Gyatso reached over and held her hand, thrilling her. 'We can go to the Vatican before dinner,' he said. 'Have you been to the Vatican? No? My hotel is just next door to it.'

Matt finished a late lunch of pasta verdi and contemplated a cappuccino. All the dairy he'd had in France didn't seem to have hurt him much, and before turning vegan he had so loved cappuccinos. He should have an espresso, he told himself. But when in Rome—. He felt maybe he should indulge a bit. The sun was shining on the blank marble wall outside the window. Judy had emailed: *don't bother wasting your life trying to help shithead humans. they only let you down. only nature matters. only nature deserves help.* Keera had emailed: *Remember Steve Earle. The revolution starts now.* And a human rights group that he had emailed this morning had written back, saying they had openings if he wanted to work on urban homelessness.

He wanted to come to some clarity. Soup kitchens. No. The bookstore wasn't a bad option. If, every now and then, he went somewhere—to do something, be of help. What kind of help? He thought of Sharada, out in some village in Nepal, empowering women. He could hardly imagine what that was like. She no longer listened to him the way she used to, when they were in college. She no longer looked at him with a request in her eyes, seeking his confirmation. He supposed there was nothing he could teach her any more. He wasn't like her: he was soft; he was useless. Damn. Damn. Damn. He beckoned the waiter, and dared himself to say, *'Uno cappuccino?'*

There was no resisting Gyatso when he reached over after dinner, leading her by the hand out of the restaurant and upstairs, to his room at his pension. The moment the door closed, they were joined in a kiss. Sharada had never slept with a man younger than she. Gyatso's hands slid down her spine, sending a shiver of pleasure through all of her: 'Oh.' His chest and shoulders were hard, muscular, through his shirt. She wondered, briefly, if it was safe to have sex with a stranger. She had never done such a thing before. Did Gyatso really find her attractive? He pressed into her, and she pulled him on to the narrow single bed, filled with desire. He pulled up her sweater, felt her waist, ribs, breasts. She moaned, slipped her hands into his shirt. His back was lovely, smooth. In no time they struggled out of their pants. Off went her panties. His bare legs were extremely shapely. He reached for a condom on the bedside table. Put it on. Positioned her. Put his thighs inside hers. She gasped as he entered, then again, again. His hands were strong on her body. Was this safe? A perfect stranger. Gyatso. Gyatso what? Gyatso Tenzing. He was delicious. Divine. Like a sex god. 'Oh, fuck.' The world was a spasm of pleasure. She bucked. She writhed. She cried out loud. Gyatso collapsed on to her. 'Oh I love this, I love this, I love this.'

'I never thought of you,' Matt said fondly, the next morning, 'as a slut. Remind me to revise my view.'

'He took me to the Coliseum, the Pantheon, the Vatican, and the Spanish Steps,' Sharada boasted, grinning. 'He's a hunk. And he's—.' She didn't say it.

'What?'

'He's amazing in bed.'

'No wonder you've been gone every day.'

They were packing in preparation to leave. A certain amount of relief had come over Matt when Sharada had called the night before, saying she would not be back till morning. When she had come, she had been glowing. And she had not felt she needed to lie to Matt about where she had spent the night.

'Is this, like, a serious thing?' Matt said, in a while. 'Do you love him or something?'

'Don't be so bourgeois.'

'Touché.' He laughed.

'We're thinking we might hook up in India some time.'

They checked out, and loaded their bags into the taxi.

'So I decided…' Matt said as they set off for the station.

'The Trevi fountain,' Sharada cut in, pointing at carvings of horses and men. She stared at the fountain till it fell out of view, then turned back to Matt. 'Sorry. Go on.'

He told her about Keera's state-to-state activism. 'They just spent a month in Montana protesting the mining laws. I'm not a Trot, I do prefer anarchism, but I was thinking… They're going to Idaho next to rally for pro-choice legislation. I thought I'd take a week off and go help out.'

'Idaho?'

'Hey, I'm from Cummington, remember?'

She grinned. 'That's more obscure than where I'm from.'

'Cummington's not so bad,' he said.

But Sharada was thinking of Khajuraho.

On the train ride back to Paris they discussed the growing class polarizations in the US, the lessons of Central America and the resurgence of leftist politics in South America, handily avoiding any discussion about how they felt about each other. Two American-bred leftists, Sharada thought: what we have in common is an impulse to altruism. Matt, for his part, realized: we get along well enough when we're not talking about ourselves.

'I'm glad we did this,' he said as Paris approached. 'It was helpful. I've had a bitch of a time.'

She agreed: 'It was just what I needed, this trip.'

Parting at the Gare du Sud, they hugged and kissed.

'Take it easy,' Matt said. 'Keep in touch.'

'Yeah,' Sharada said. 'Write me all about what you get up to.'

They parted outside, on the platform.

'Bye,' he said.

'Bye,' she said.

They never so much as emailed each other again.

The Girl of No Age

~

Politely, Rabindra had asked the woman at the door whether she would let him in to take pictures from the top floor. Her house was well located, he had explained: the king's funeral procession would be passing by in an hour, and he needed an unobstructed view. There was a camera bag slung across his shoulders and a tripod in his hands. She had looked him up and down, and allowed him in.

This is what Rabindra told me last week as we sat in his courtyard looking at his photographs of the funeral. His wife, Rashmi, served us coffee, but did not join us. When they had married three years ago, I had cut Rabindra off. Perhaps Rashmi resented that. I too felt uneasy around her, and had no real desire to get to know her. I did not want any new relationships at this point in my life.

'It turned out she was my childhood friend,' Rabindra said, about the woman whose house he had entered. 'We grew up together in the village, our family houses were like this.' He pointed at his chair, then at mine. 'We recognized each other only as soon as I stepped in. It was her face—and the way she carried herself. I saw a flash of my childhood friend in her, and she also recognized me at exactly the same time.' He laughed. 'We were both amazed.'

Later, after the funeral procession had passed by, she had asked him to stay on for tea. He had met her son and daughter-in-law, and also her husband, who was, as it turned out, a man who had been arrested in an infamous case, decades ago, on charges of idol smuggling. 'There was that scandal, remember?' Rabindra said. 'We were in college. He would have gone to jail, but his connections saved him.' He laughed again. 'My childhood friend had become the wife of an idol smuggler!'

The gardener who was tending Rabindra's garden, who had been stooped over a flowerbed nearby, stood at this time, and stretched his back. Then he walked over to a wicker table at the other side of the garden, and examined a chessboard set out on a table there.

I said, 'That's quite trusting, for an idol smuggler's wife to let a stranger into her house.'

'The king's death did that to people,' Rabindra said. 'Everyone was opening up to others. Besides, most people, you know, are quite trusting.'

It depends on how you approach them, I wanted to say, but I didn't. Maybe if you ask in the right way, people let you into their houses. Or if they refuse to, it won't matter, because if you are the kind of person who asks strangers to let you into their house, you are the kind of person who would not mind if they said no.

'More coffee?' he said.

I asked, 'Is there more in the pot?'

As he refilled my cup, I told him—although he already knew

it—that his gardener, Shiva, who was still examining the chessboard, used to work for my husband and me. Shiva had not been good with flowers but he had kept the hedges trimmed, and he was pleasant. I was working at Save then, but when I was free I used to talk to him. In our exchanges we would take each plant so seriously, discussing its growth and how it had fared under our various experiments with bone-meal, dung, nitrogen. I had wanted to cover my husband's compound walls with creepers. Shiva had preferred perennials to seasonal blooms. We had made a project out of a rose vine with the deepest blood-red buds.

I used to have the time, back then, to sit around and chat like that. Or I had the inclination to. I used to ask Shiva about his wife and children in the village, and he used to invite me to come and meet them. His village was only an hour's drive outside Kathmandu. I would say yes, I'd like to meet your family, and I would suggest it to my husband: but we were always too busy to go.

Over the years, I don't know if I changed or Shiva changed, but our relationship changed. I began to cram my time with work as my husband got angrier, and I saw Shiva less and less frequently. My conversations with him grew perfunctory. By the time I had had my second miscarriage we had stopped discussing the plants. He would ask for money to buy some fertilizer and I would give it to him. Or I would tell him that I liked, or didn't like, his latest experiments. That was how our relationship became. I began to give him tea money instead of offering him tea when I made some. He knew I was not happy in my marriage. Sometimes he tried to restore our earlier friendship by chiding me: 'What's this, you never have time to see how your garden is doing.' I would agree that this was no way to live. But some compulsion had taken hold of me. All I wanted to do was work.

Rabindra's house, adjacent to the courtyard where we were sitting, was newly built. He told me his photographs of the king's funeral had earned him a tidy profit. The photographs lay scattered on the table before us: hordes of confused, angry people, chary-eyed officials, funeral pyres. I told Rabindra that I had been in the crowds that day, waiting for the funeral procession to pass by. When it did, I hadn't been able to see the king's face. 'It didn't matter,' I said. 'I went just to be part of the crowd, part of what was happening.' It had felt like madness to stay in my apartment at that time. I didn't say that to Rabindra. I said, 'It's so far away already. The king's death.'

'We forget things so fast.'

'Some things.'

We both smiled, because we realized we were talking about our marriages.

It didn't bother me that we weren't talking directly about all that had passed. Instead it felt kind, forgiving. It wasn't as though Rabindra and I could ever be close again. I don't know why I married my husband. Rabindra and I were not lovers, but we were good friends through college, back when it was unusual for male and female students to talk at all. We were both studying law, but I wanted to enter the NGO world, and he wanted to be a photographer. It was he who introduced me to the man who would be my husband. Rabindra left law school and went to work for him. Later he quit and opened his own photo studio. My husband was already pursuing me then.

I think I married him because I felt, as I reached my mid-twenties, that I should be married; and Rabindra's family was pressuring him to marry a woman of their choosing. The caste difference between us seemed an unsurmountable obstacle then. Of course it wouldn't have been. We lacked the imagination, or the courage to love. Or we were too young to try. Almost immediately after I agreed to marry the man who became my husband, I felt pierced through with grief. I had lost my best friend, and the life we could have had together.

Perhaps my husband and Rabindra still meet sometimes, I don't know. I stopped meeting Rabindra when—upon the failure of his first marriage—he took a second wife, Rashmi. His first wife had refused to sign the divorce papers. He had two daughters by that marriage. He left them all and moved in with Rashmi, legalizing their bond through the tricks and loopholes of our legal system. After a time the scandal died down; everyone accepted what had happened. I might have accepted it, too, had I not been shaken by convulsions in my own marriage.

Over coffee, Rabindra behaved as affably as ever, as though we had never stopped meeting each other or being friends. But so much was new in us, almost too much to share. He couldn't possibly be the same person he had been. I wasn't the same person I used to be.

I still worked at Save, expanding health care into rural areas, but our work had become harder, meaner. The insurgency that escalated after the king's death changed everything. Last year, for the first time, the Maoists and the army began to clash in our project areas, and this changed me. In a village I went to, to set up polio vaccinations, I met a family whose daughter had been taken out of her house in the middle of the night by the army. She had been blindfolded, dragged to the village centre, told to run and shot while running, even as her family members looked on. She had been reported as an armed Maoist who had died in combat. I spent weeks crying after I returned from that village, not because I didn't know that this could happen, that people could kill children in war. The daily papers were filled with such incidents. What shook me was that the girl's parents, speaking to me in a daze, couldn't remember how old their daughter had been. The mother had said the girl was nine. The father had said ten. The other villagers, who had gathered around to hear the story retold, had said the girl was at most twelve. She had been studying in class two: that was the only objective measure we could find to go by.

When I returned from that trip I returned to my estranged husband—not out of love, but out of terror. I could not bear the thought of the girl of no age. I needed his—or somebody's—physical proximity. I needed to touch a body filled with life. I needed, too, to feel that somebody knew me, and could tell others about me if I were to suddenly die.

For a while, after his initial resentment eased, it was all right between us. We talked as we used to, years ago, and we even laughed at each other's jokes. We did not mention the possibility of trying again for a child, but the question hung there between us, unanswered. We visited a few friends together. One day we went on a picnic like teenage lovers.

But within a few months his anger returned. He never actually beat me. The most he did was throw things around, break a glass, shout, call me names. It was enough to paralyse me with fear. Earlier, I felt I had disappointed him and I sought to placate him. It had taken me years to see that his rage would not die, that his rage was his power. This time I did not wait.

Two months ago I left him for good. I put up with one final screaming, then left. I have not seen him since; I have not spoken to him on the phone. I have thrown away all my photographs of him. Legally he is still my husband. I do not know if I have the strength to confront him, to file for divorce.

It was by pure coincidence that I ran into Rabindra last week. We passed each other, then he called out to me, recognizing me through the years. I did not know he had moved into a new house. 'Come, it's right here, let's have some fresh coffee,' he said in his easy way, the way he used to talk to me, back in college. He said, 'I'll show you my photographs. The photographs that bought me my house.'

Meeting him again, and meeting Shiva, the gardener, I was reminded of all the mistakes I had made; but I also felt forgiven, a bit. To sit in a garden, drinking coffee. We were the lucky ones. I think if I had said this to Rabindra he would have understood. He and I—people like us—we had made mistakes, but had had a chance to correct them. Or others had made mistakes in our lives, and we had had a chance to survive them.

My sorrows are manageable. What I had last week, those moments in Rabindra's courtyard, I was grateful for. The sky seemed very clear, and the air charged and bright. Life felt open, intensely so. I felt like I should—like it is my sacred task—to move unafraid into the emptiness.

After the coffee I came back to my apartment and began to unpack at last. For two months I had been living out of my suitcase. That day I took my clothes out of my suitcases and hung them in the built-in closet. On the window ledge I put up photographs of my parents and brother's family. I put a plant in the sitting room. Rabindra had given me a picture of the dead king. For a long while I held it in my hands, and looked at it. And I thought: the woman who had let Rabindra into her house—surely it occurred to her that this stranger could be dangerous? Her husband was an idol smuggler. An unknown person at the door might have brought trouble.

But perhaps most people, as Rabindra says, are quite trusting.

That night, cooking my first meal in the apartment, I thought—at what age did I grow difficult?

My relationship with the gardener, for example. Was it Shiva who changed or I? As my husband got angrier I became more and more frenetic at Save, expanding our projects into new districts—for unlike at life, I was good at my work. I felt bothered by Shiva, and no longer wanted to talk about, say, the tenacity of mint roots. Shiva also stopped making an effort with me. When we met at all, he would ask if I knew other people needing a gardener, or whether I knew of offices looking to hire. He would ask for a raise, for more money for tea, for a loan of a few thousand. It wearied me. I began to avoid him, and over time—after a few years—I no longer had to meet him because I moved out. By the time I moved back in with my husband, he had quit.

When I saw him last week, after I recognized him—for he had aged a little—he said, 'You never came to the village to meet my family.'

I asked after his wife and children, and he asked after my

health, and for a while it was all right. I felt we could be friends again if we wanted.

Just as I could grow close again to Rabindra if I wanted. For Rashmi's sake I will not pursue this. I once loved him. I am drawn to him still, or to my idea of him. And I am lonely. I recognize the potential to cause damage.

And actually I do not want him; what I want is to be like him. I want the gall, the gumption—for that is what it takes—to ask people I do not know if I may come into their lives, without fearing that they might say no, or fearing that once they let me in, they might hurt me. I want to know, truly know, others, reach out to people who would otherwise just come and go, passing through my life as strangers.

Credits and Acknowledgements

~

'Heera Maharjan Loses His Way' originally appeared in *Tampa Review*. 'Friends' originally appeared in *Jungle Planet and Other Stories*. 'Love Marriage' originally appeared in *An Other Voice*, 'Diesel' and 'I Don't Like Shanta Khanal' originally appeared in *The Journal*. 'Three Hundred Rupees' originally appeared in *Himal Southasian*. 'The Eldest Son Thinks of Home', 'Soar', 'The Student in Love', and 'The Secretary of the Student Union Makes a Career Choice' originally appeared in *Artful Dodge*. 'Ta'Angzoum among the Cows' originally appeared in *Studies in Nepali History and Society*. 'Tilled Earth' originally appeared in *Bellingham Review*.

These stories were written over the course of a decade, in between Kathmandu and Seattle. I am grateful to innumerable friends on whom I have leaned, at times very heavily, during this period. Khushwant Singh enabled me to give this collection final form in Kasauli, India, in 2005, during a turbulent time in Nepal. Ben Schonveld and Bronwyn Hudson housed me in Kathmandu during the final edit. My deep thanks to them all. Over the years, Ravi Singh has greatly nurtured my fiction, as have Wayne Amtzis and Kesang Tseten in Kathmandu, Joel

Isaacson (latterly in Santa Cruz), Tej Thapa (mostly) in the Netherlands, and Maya Sonenberg and Shawn Wong in Seattle. My immense gratitude to them. Thank you to Basanta Bidari of the Lumbini Development Trust for orienting me to Lumbini: if there are any misrepresentations in my story, these are of course my own fault. I am grateful to Daniel Lak for helping me make room for fiction in the hurly-burly of real life. And my abiding love to Bhekh Bahadur and Rita Thapa, Bhaskar and Sumira, Barune, Maya, Siddhant, and again, my sister Tej. Brilliance.